CLOSELY WATCHED TRAINS

CLOSELY WATCHED TRAINS

Bohumil Hrabal

Translated by Edith Pargeter

With a Foreword by JOSEF ŠKVORECKÝ

Northwestern University Press
Evanston, Illinois

Northwestern University Press
Evanston, Illinois 60201

First published 1965 as *Ostře sledované vlaky* by Česko-
slovenský Spisovatel, Prague. Copyright © 1965 by
Bohumil Hrabal. English translation copyright © 1968
by Jonathan Cape Ltd. First published 1968 by Jonathan
Cape Ltd. as *A Close Watch on the Trains*. Sphere Books Ltd
Abacus edition of *Closely Observed Trains* published 1990.
Northwestern University Press paperback edition of
Closely Watched Trains published 1990 by arrangement
with Macdonald & Company. Foreword by Josef
Škvorecký. Copyright © Viking Penguin Inc., 1981.
Foreword reprinted by arrangement with Viking Penguin
Inc.

Printed in the United States of America

The paper used in this publication meets the minimum
requirements of American National Standard for Infor-
mation Sciences—Permanence of Paper for Printed Library Materials, ANSI Z39.48-1984

Library of Congress Cataloging-in-Publication Data

Hrabal, Bohumil, 1914–
    [Ostře sledované vlaky. English]
    Closely watched trains / Bohumil Hrabal ; translated by Edith
Pargeter ; with a foreword by Josef Skvorecky.
        p.   cm.
    Translation of: Ostře sledované vlaky.
    Reprint with new introd. Originally published: Closely observed
trains. London : Sphere Books, 1990.
    ISBN 0-8101-0857-7 (pbk.)
    I. Pargeter, Edith, 1913–   . II. Škvorecký, Josef. III. Title.
IV. Title: Closely observed trains.
PG5039.18.R20813   1990
891.8'635—dc20   90-45393
                                                              CIP

CONTENTS

FOREWORD

by Josef Škvorecký

"Woe betide the country that needs heroes."
—Bertolt Brecht, *Galileo Galilei*

WESTERN readers can readily understand Bohumil Hrabal even if they know nothing whatsoever about socialist realism, but without such knowledge—and I mean a knowledge of its history, not of its theory, for socialist realism has no theory worth taking seriously—people in the West can scarcely appreciate Hrabal's status in Czechoslovakia, where he is considered almost a national hero, a revolutionary of prose, an innovator, a revitalizer of language: in short, a man who has opened up new vistas for Czech writing, who has extricated it from the vicious circle of propaganda and set it back on the path of art. The story of an adolescent boy with an intimate personal problem who commits an act of heroism that is more a consequence of sexual euphoria than premeditated patriotism is undeniably an original work from the hand of a master storyteller. American literature, however, has a long tradition of what might be called deliberate "deheroization" of war—ranging from the ingenuous *The Red Badge of Courage* through Frederick Henry's valorous deeds while eating cheese, right down to Joseph Heller's *Catch-22*, and, for all I know, to works even less reverential—and therefore I'm not entirely certain that the tragicomedy of Miloš Hrma will seem bold enough in content and innovative enough in form to make Hrabal's apotheosis wholly comprehensible to the Western reader. I'm afraid one simply has to know the basic facts—not the theory—of socialist realism.

When William Dean Howells was preaching realism, he advised American writers to concentrate on "the rosier aspects of American life, because they are the more American." He could have had no idea at the time that he was in fact articulating the starting point for a category of art that took power (yes, "took power" rather than "appeared": *hat die Macht ergriffen*) much later and in another country altogether. In the beginning this category was genuinely intended to be no more than an emphasis on the "rosier aspects" of Soviet life, or, translated into Communist party cant: The old-style realism of the critical or bourgeois variety, despite frequently harsh criticism, was fundamentally just recording the status quo; socialist realism was supposed to present reality not merely as it actually was at the moment but also "in its revolutionary development and perspectives." In plain terms, reality was to be painted pink.

Whatever Maksim Gorky meant when he introduced the term to the Soviet public, the party bureaucrats—men whom Aleksandr Dovzhenko, in his diary, labeled "cutthroats, know-nothings," and, most frequently, "dog-turds"—understood Gorky's ruminations on socialist realism as a call to eliminate from the reality of socialism anything that might cast a shadow over the rosy hues: first, any social criticism of the postrevolutionary status quo, and second, aspects that they considered "decadent and offensive to socialist morality," mainly violent death (except death in the grand heroic mode) and sex (except Victorian-style innuendo). In the late stages of Stalinism things became so confusing that these "decadent" human affairs were even censored out of translated novels of social criticism from the capitalist world. The late Warren Miller—who was certainly no capitalist lackey—never could understand why the Czech translation of *The Cool World,* his novel about the Harlem contemporaries of Miloš Hrma and one of the last books to be written in the classical Marxist tradition of social criticism, was banned in Communist Czechoslovakia in 1962. The answer was that since it was quite impossible to expurgate sex from the lives of Harlem teenagers, the book was dumped. (It was actually printed but never released to the general public; a very limited edition was distributed to "trusted pedagogues and specialists.") The banning of *The Cool World* occurred only two years before Hrabal submitted the first draft of *Closely Watched Trains* to his publisher.

Perhaps it will now be somewhat clearer to the uninitiated why a story combining *ejaculatio praecox* and anti-Nazi sabotage hit the Victorianized and sex-starved Czechoslovak market like a bomb. A far less explicit blending of the sexual drive with wartime heroism led my own book *The Cowards* to be seized by the censor seven years earlier, setting in motion a landslide of bans that buried Hrabal's first collection of short stories, *Pearls on the Bottom (Perličky na dně),* which was withdrawn a week before publication. *Closely Watched Trains,* however, did not appear until 1965, in a period when the "thaw" was well under way, when the Stalinists were keeping a low profile and their literary and moralistic dogmas were no longer taken seriously. Moreover, *Closely Watched Trains* appeared in a form that from the censor's point of view was far more publishable than its original version, which Hrabal had written in 1949, a year after the Communist takeover, when he was still very much an underground writer.

Sometime in 1950 Hrabal read this original version, called *The Legend of Cain,* at a gathering of an underground literary circle to which I also belonged. The circle used to meet in the flat of poet and artist Jiří Kolář, best known in the West today for his collages. It was there that I first listened to the dark tale of an existentially motivated suicide attempt that had taken place in a hotel in the midst of an apocalyptic war. Hrabal did not publish this original version of the story until 1968, the year of the Prague Spring, in a volume entitled *Macabrosa and Legends (Moritáty a legendy).* It has not been republished since.

There is a great deal less sex in *The Legend of Cain,* and to the extent that it is there, the narrator has no particular problem with it. On the other hand, the story does contain a great many ordinary human deaths that have nothing to do with heroism. Shortly after delivering the coup de grace to a mortally wounded German soldier, the narrator himself is shot by a Czech guard. This absurd ending, more typical of Albert Camus than of laureates of the Stalin Prize, is very unlike the socially significant demise of Miloš Hrma in *Closely Watched Trains.* Cain and the main characters of *The Legend of Cain* are utterly obsessed with death. The doctor who, in *Closely Watched Trains,* advises Miloš how to deal with his sexual problem commits suicide in *The Legend of Cain* by tying himself up— and it is not clear whether the narrator helped him in this—and jumping into a furnace: "Before the furnace a huddled black puppet was lying. It was charred all over, and its right eye, molten and fallen out of the skull, was staring at me. When I walked down a few steps, it burst open and began flowing out quietly on the floor."

The novella's black imagination reaches a peak with the hero's vision of a "beautiful suicide" worthy of the imagination of Edgar Allan Poe, in the terms of socialist realism an archdecadent who even appealed to Fyodor Dostoevsky: "I knew a religious man who craved for holiness so much that one night he lifted the lid of a crypt in the local church, and, having entangled himself in the shrouds and in the petrified intestines of that holy woman, he shot himself through the head and at the same time closed the lid so that he was not found until years later. Until he looked almost like that saint." The novella is bursting with such "unacceptable" passages. Moreover, Hrabal had not written it right after the war but after the Communist putsch in 1948, and it may not be irrelevant to recall that in Czechoslovakia that was the beginning of an era of "class liquidation" and "layered graves," as they were called: The executed, because there were so many of them, were buried one on top of the other, in layers, to save space. It was also a time when the police chauffeur responsible for scattering over the roads of north Bohemia the ashes of those twelve innocent men hung after the Rudolf Slanský trial quipped in the canteen of the Ministry of the Interior that he'd never been able to fit twelve men into his car before. If there is any genuinely morbid postwar prose from Czechoslovakia, then *The Legend of Cain* is it. I would prefer, however, to say that the age itself was morbid. Good literature merely reflected that morbidity.

Despite the "thaw," then, *The Legend of Cain* was still too strong a book for 1965, and so Hrabal, in his own words (*Macabrosa and Legends*), "wove a braid" from it called *Closely Watched Trains*. Something of the horrors of *The Legend of Cain* remains—the cruel things done to animals, for instance—and Hrabal added others: the stories of the nurse, Beatrice, who eases badly burned German soldiers into death and of the charwoman who cleans up the blood after executions. Nevertheless, it was an essentially different book, and it became the best-seller of the 1960s.

Many of Hrabal's old friends, particularly those who remained staunch nonconformists despite the liberalizing trend, were disappointed. They called *Closely Watched Trains* "prettied-up" Hrabal and regretted that the author had gone so far out of his way to appeal to conventional taste. I myself am not sure who is right, but two things seem beyond dispute. Formally, *Closely Watched Trains* is smoother, more masterfully executed than the raw *Legend of Cain*. The author took what was essentially a linear story, despite some flashbacks, and subjected it to what Joseph Conrad called "deliberate confusion," or, if you like, Hrabal formally modernized it, though he did return to the chronological mode in the film scenario of *Closely Watched Trains*. On the other hand, it is also beyond dispute that, for all its freshness and originality, *Closely Watched Trains* presents a far more conventional literary representation of war than the Boschian visions of *The Legend of Cain*. This difference, perhaps, can best be made clear in a key scene that occurs in both stories, in which Cain and Miloš are held hostage on the munitions train and confronted by the scarred S.S. captain. In *The Legend of Cain* this officer allows Cain to get off the train without noticing his scarred wrist:

His narrow lips were seeking, in the last moment when everything would soon be lost, some object for which he

would be forgiven. . . . I saw . . . that he knew I was not
his enemy, but that I was his lucky chance, his good
deed, which, perhaps, Providence would weigh up on its
scales. . . . Besides, it was disagreeable today to sully the
agreeable end of war. . . . He was smiling. His brutal
soul received the first candy, and he was drunk with
magnanimity. . . . I told myself: I am grateful to you,
devil, because I accept my life from your hands. I am
forced to declare you to be my angel. You are my God.
. . . [The two S.S. men] threw down some cigarettes after
me and smiled at me. Because why should they be angry
when the commander is not? Why should they butcher
me when the commander, out of perversity, does not
wish me butchered?

This is a straight, dispassionate, and rugged treat-
ment of a harsh war experience. The captain is not a
man who, mellowed by the horrors of battle, is reminded of a common humanity. He is not made human by any sentimental solidarity with another
comrade in death. He remains the whimsical, inscru-
table Nazi. Compare how differently the same man
with the dueling scar appears in *Closely Watched Trains:*

The captain's eyes were gazing now at my wrist, where I,
too, had a scar. . . . Perhaps this captain had already
learned much more, perhaps he was looking at everything now from the opposite viewpoint, and his eyes . . .
were all staring at my wrist, and the captain stretched
out his little whip, and with it drew back my other
sleeve, too, and looked at the second scar. *"Kamerad,"*
he said.

One can see why the nonconformist critics called
this "braid" of a story a "prettifying" of Hrabal and
of reality. Indeed, shifts like these smack dangerously
of humanitarian, if not downright sentimental,
clichés, of which Hrabal's early prose was remarkably

free. One can sense that Hrabal was aware of what had happened to him, for in a self-deprecating conclusion to a later book of his called *The Buds* (*Poupata*) he wrote:

A cabdriver . . . drove me this year from the Barrandov studios, and suddenly he laughed and asked me, "Aren't you Mr. Hrabal?"
 I replied, "Indeed I am."
 And he said, "Ha, ha, they've outsmarted you, haven't they? You wanted to be a *poète maudit,* and they've turned you into a socialist realist. That's what I call a real achievement."

The nonconformist avant-garde, then, saw *Closely Watched Trains* as "prettied-up" Hrabal, but this harsh criticism of a best-seller must be understood in the context of the time and the country. Because an oppressive regime is always most unjust toward the creators of all sorts of "*Entartete Kunst,*" the avant-garde has a tendency to be unfair in its judgment of those whom the oppressive regime, however hesitatingly, tolerates. It is a narrow-minded view, and in the democratic world one can afford to be more liberal. Here, the small compromises one makes do not play into the hands of some party cultural secretary who would be happier if there were no writers and no culture at all, just hacks and an entertainment industry.
 Objectively, I don't think there can be much doubt that, compared to the dark and often excessively encoded and private world of *The Legend of Cain, Closely Watched Trains* is a generally more accessible and dazzling display of storytelling. It still contains quite enough of human death, but here Hrabal balances it, as he does not in *The Legend of Cain,* with something no less human, something that has annulled death for

generation after generation: sex or, if you prefer, love—its splendor, its despair (as embodied in the stationmaster), and its evenly matched battle (so far) with the angel of Thanatos. I would say that in the literature of the so-called socialist states, *Closely Watched Trains* is, as far as I know, the only genuinely successful, genuinely persuasive "optimistic tragedy." In this sense it achieves what Gorky may have had in mind, and what Dovzhenko's "dog-turds" never have and never will understand. Witness the fate of Jiří Menzel's film version of *Closely Watched Trains*: awarded an Oscar for Best Foreign Film of 1967, banned after the Soviet invasion of Czechoslovakia, and never re-released. Witness also the fact that as I write this foreword, there has still not been a reprinting of the novella. Moreover, unlike *The Legend of Cain, Closely Watched Trains* has that blend of tragedy and humor that is so typical of life in Central Europe.

Humor of a sometimes rather bawdy variety is inherent in the very names of the characters, which unabashedly belong to the tradition—or, if you like, the convention—of symbolic nomenclature. Miloš Hrma might be translated as Sweetheart Cunt-Hair; Hubička means Tender Kiss; Zdenička Svatá (she is called Virginia in the translation) is Saint Sidonia; Viktoria Freie elicits associations of Victorious Freedom, both in the general sense of the expression as it would have been used by resistance fighters and in Miloš's own private sense; moreover, the Czech pronunciation of the word Freie (*freye*) suggests a sexual and alcoholic frolic. Sex is thus a main source of humor, as it usually is and has always been, from *The Canterbury Tales* to *The Good Soldier Švejk*.

Here we must avoid the tendency to simplify as displayed by some Western reviewers who, familiar with only a few internationally well-known types from the "lesser literatures of the world," resort to labels rather than to analysis. For such reviewers, every Czech writer who displays even a modicum of humor is writing in "the Švejkian tradition." Pasting that label on Hrabal's work—and here it is the short stories rather than *Closely Watched Trains* that are a case in point—would be only slightly more accurate than describing William Faulkner as "Twainian" because they both use folksy material.

A comparison with Faulkner is, by the way, more appropriate here. Leaving aside Hrabal's deliberate tributes to the American author, such as his novel *Dance Lessons for the Advanced and the Elderly* (*Taneční hodiny pro starši a pokročilé*), written in a single, endless sentence, Hrabal, like Faulkner, is a blend of "low" and "high": The folkloric material is filtered through a sophisticated intellect. Hrabal, who has a doctorate in law, also has a typically "American" biography: He has been a traveling salesman, a steelworker, a dealer in scrap paper, a stagehand. He married a charming waitress who appears to have stepped right out of his stories, and he stylizes himself as a beer drinker who thinks like an intellectual but talks the language of the common man. His storytelling style, which Hrabal himself refers to as "*pábení*" (the closest English equivalent would probably be "palavering"), is very much like Faulkner's (again I'm speaking of Hrabal's short stories) in *The Hamlet,* drawn from sources akin to the humorous style of Mark Twain or Ambrose Bierce; many of Hrabal's characters are not-so-distant relatives of Paul Bunyan, Davy Crockett, or Pecos Bill. A number of scenes in Hrabal's stories—like the frightened flight of the pony through Mrs. Littlejohn's home in *The Hamlet*—exploit the art of the silent-film gag. Hrabal, by the way, has something more in common with those early film comedies: He is read with equal delight by people unspoiled by literary knowledge and by college professors.

Hrabal's life story is typical of that of a writer who hides a lyrical tangle of nerves beneath a tough, Hemingway exterior. As such, of course, he is a misfit in socialist society, at least in the kind that existed in his country under the Nazis and exists today under the neo-Stalinists. He went unpublished during the 1950s, although everyone knowledgeable in Prague was aware of his existence, until 1956, when Jiří Kolář assumed the risk of issuing a semilegal, not-for-sale Bibliophile Club edition of Hrabal's story "Conversations with People."

When that strange socialism imported into Czechoslovakia from the Russian empire began to take on a slightly more human face, Hrabal became a literary star. The most important thing about him, however, was that he personified an ideal quality, one that Aleksandr Solzhenitsyn ascribes to Alexsandr Tvardovsky in his memoirs, *The Oak and the Calf*: He became "a writer of the people . . . he wrote as freely as one breathes." Naturally, Hrabal supported Alexander Dubček and his ill-fated experiment with socialism in 1968. Consequently, after the Soviet invasion, when Dubček's now deposed parliamentary chairman, the populist leader Josef Smrkovský, attended Hrabal's private birthday party, the secret police got their hooks into Hrabal. The poet's nerves did not hold out, and the result was a prolonged and critical period of hospitalization. Then he broke, or rather bent somewhat, as so many before him had done. He publicly declared his support for "socialism," which he took pains not to define—and how many different socialisms exist in the world today?—and he signed the "Anti-Charter," a document forced upon the creative community by the Czechoslovak regime as a reaction to Charter 77, the human-rights manifesto issued by many of his old friends. As a reward, the regime has officially published, so far, three new books by him. One is a collection of literary fragments; another is a charmingly idealized portrait of his mother, free of any explicitly sexual or existential connotations; and the third encountered the same fate as *The Legend of Cain,* except in a far more drastic form. *The Town Where Time Stopped* is philosophically not far removed from *The Legend of Cain,* but for the Prague edition, published as *The Beauty of Sadness* (the original manuscript was published under its original title without the author's permission by an exile publishing house), Hrabal altered his characteristically spontaneous diction so that, as the popular definition of socialist realism runs, "even the comrades from the Central Committee would understand it." Worst of all, he completely eliminated a long and powerful conclusion containing the book's main message. The passage is in fact a lyrical requiem, delivered in strong, Waughian tones, for the world of beauty, which, in the perversion of "class justice," has been destroyed by the "new world"—that is, by Communism. This requiem culminates in a poetic report on the state of the author's soul during his "illness" after 1968, when he thought long about what he would still like to write:

Beloved, this first (and future) book of mine, will be borne gently by the sensuous dynamics of Matisse's *Luxe, calme et voluptée.* . . . It will be suffused with the brilliant pigment of light and space. The second book will be called *Surprise in the Woods,* and it will be full of fear and stress and vain efforts to adapt, like (Edvard) Munch's lyrical

xviii

expressionism. In it I shall attempt something I have been thinking about for many years, something that, deriving from realistic drawings, gradually moves toward a state of deformation and at last becomes something that is the essence of action painting, as practiced by Jackson Pollock.

I don't know whether Hrabal has written this work yet or not. If the situation in Prague, described by Heinrich Böll as "the graveyard of culture," persists, I am afraid that this story will join the other manuscripts in Hrabal's desk drawer—the best of his manuscripts: *The Town Where Time Stopped, I Served the King of England, Too Loud a Solitude.*

(1981)

TRANSLATED FROM THE CZECH BY PAUL WILSON

BY this year, the year 'forty-five, the Germans had already lost command of the air-space over our little town. Over the whole region, in fact, and for that matter, the whole country. The dive-bombers were disrupting communications to such an extent that the morning trains ran at noon, the noon trains in the evening, and the evening trains during the night, so that now and then it might happen that an afternoon train came in punctual to the minute, according to the time-table, but only because it was the morning passenger train running four hours late.

Just the day before yesterday an enemy fighter shot up a German pursuit plane over our town, and blew one wing clean off it; and then the fuselage burned out, and crashed somewhere out in the fields. But this wing, as it tore loose from the fuselage, ripped out a few handfuls of screws and nuts to spatter down over the square and peck at the heads of several women there, and the wing itself went on hovering over the town, and everybody who could stood and watched it, right to the moment when it swooped lower with a creaky motion just above the square. All the customers came tumbling out from both the restaurants, as the shadow of this wing hung rocking above the square, and everybody who was watching it went rushing across from one side to the other, and then back again to where they'd been standing a minute before, because the wing kept on swinging like a gigantic pendulum, sending them all scuttling in the opposite direction from where it looked as if it was going to fall, and all the time it was grinding out a crescendo clatter and a whining song. And then suddenly it hurtled down and crashed into the deanery garden.

And within five minutes our townspeople had made a clean sweep of all the plates and sheet-metal from this wing, and the pieces reappeared the very next day as little roofs for rabbit-hutches and hen-houses; in fact one man spent that same afternoon cutting out patterns from this plundered sheet-metal, and in the evening he made them into beautiful leg-guards for motor-bikes. In this way not only the wing vanished, but also all the parts and plates from the fuselage of the German plane, which had crashed outside the town, in the snow-covered fields.

I went out there on my bicycle to have a look, half an hour after the dog-fight. And all along the road I kept meeting people from the town, pulling hand-carts loaded with the stuff they'd looted. It was a job to guess what use they could possibly make of some of that junk. But I went pedalling on, all I wanted was to have a look at the smashed plane. I couldn't stand acquisitive people, and I wasn't interested in prising off odd parts and grabbing at bits of rubbish. By this time there was a regular path trodden through the snow all the way to that black wreckage, and along this path my father came marching, carrying a sort of silver musical instrument, and grinning and brand-ishing these silvery intestines as he marched. Some kind of pipes, they looked like; and that's what they were, pipes from the aeroplane, the pipes the petrol flowed through. It was only when we were at home that evening that I realized why Dad was so delighted with this plunder. He cut those pipes up into identical pieces, and polished them, until he'd turned them into sixty shiny tubes, and then he laid alongside them his own patent propelling pencil with the retractable lead.

There wasn't anything in the world my father couldn't make, and that was because he'd been retired on pension ever since he was forty-eight. He was an engine-driver, and he'd been on locomotives from the time he turned twenty, so he had to his credit double the service time he'd actually put in. But our townspeople went green with envy when they reflected that Father might still have twenty or thirty years of life ahead of him. And on top of that, Dad went on getting up in the morning earlier than the people who were still going to work. He used to go round collecting from the whole district, wherever there was anything to be picked up, screws, horse-shoes, anything; he fetched away all manner of odd parts and useless rubbish from the public dumps, and laid everything away at home in the sheds and the attics. It always looked like a scrap-yard full of old iron at our place. And if there was any old furniture people no longer needed, our Dad would take that off their hands, too, so that at home, although there were only three of us living there, we had fifty chairs, seven tables, nine couches, and shoals of little cabinets and washstands and jugs.

And even that wasn't enough for Dad. He used to go riding off on his bicycle all round our district, and even farther afield, raking through the rubbish tips with a hook, and in the evening he'd come back with his haul, because he said there wasn't anything that might not come in for something some day; and he was right, too, for when anyone needed anything that wasn't being manufactured any more, some spare part for a car, or a shredding-mill, or a threshing-machine, and couldn't get hold of what he wanted, he came along to our place, and Father considered for a moment, and then set off from memory for some particular spot in the loft or the shed, or prowled round the pile of stuff in our yard, and then he rummaged in there somewhere, and in a few moments he hauled out some piece of scrap that would really do the job. That was why my father was always put in charge of the 'Iron Sunday' scrap collections; and when he carted off all that assorted iron scrap to the railway station he always took it round by our gate, and tipped a little bit of his 'Iron Sunday' over into our yard.

And yet the neighbours could never forgive him. Maybe it was because of Great-grandfather Luke, who was only eighteen when he was granted a disability pension of a gold piece a day, though afterwards, in the republic, he got it in crowns.

My great-grandfather was born in the year eighteen thirty, and in eighteen forty-eight he was a drummer in the army, and as a drummer-boy he took part in the fighting on Charles Bridge. The students dug out cobble-stones from the paving there to throw at the soldiers, and they hit Great-grandfather on the knee and crippled him for life. From that time on he was granted this disability pension, a gold piece every day, and every day he spent it on a bottle of rum and two packets of tobacco, but instead of sitting quietly at home to do his drinking and smoking, he went off limping about the streets and the field paths, taking a special delight in turning up wherever there were people slaving away at some hard labour. And there he'd grin and gloat over these workers, and drink this rum of his, and smoke his tobacco, and what with one thing and another, never a year passed without Great-grandfather Luke getting beaten up somewhere, and Grandfather having to wheel him home in the wheelbarrow.

But Great-grandfather only bobbed up as fresh as ever, and was soon off again bragging about who was the better off everywhere he went, until somebody beat him up again in the same unchristian way. Until the fall of Austria put a stop to this disability pension he'd been drawing for seventy years. Until his allowance under the republic dwindled so much that it wouldn't run to his bottle of rum and his two packets of tobacco any longer.

But even then, never a year passed without somebody beating Great-grandfather Luke unconscious, because he still went on dragging himself around the district flaunting those seventy years when he'd had his bottle of rum and his tobacco every day. Until in the year nineteen thirty-five Great-grandfather did his bragging in front of some quarrymen whose stone quarry had just been closed down on them, and they beat him up so badly that he died. The doctor said he might very well have been with us a good twenty years yet. That was why there was no other family that stuck in the town's gullet like ours did.

My grandfather again, not to fall too far short of the standard set by Great-grandfather Luke, was a hypnotist who did his act in small circuses, and the whole town saw in his hypnotism nothing more nor less than an ambitious bid to stroll his way through life as idly as possible. But when the Germans crossed our frontier in March to occupy the whole country, and were advancing in the direction of Prague, our grandfather was the only one who went out to meet them, nobody else but our grandfather, and he set out to defy those Germans by means of his hypnotic powers, to hold back the advancing tanks by the force of suggestion. He went striding along the highroad with his eyes fixed on the leading tank, the spearhead of that entire motorized army. In this tank, waist-deep in the cabin, stood an officer of the Reich, with a black beret with the death's-head badge and the crossed bones on his head, and my grandfather kept on going steadily forward, straight towards this tank, with his hands stretched out, and his eyes spraying towards the Germans the thought: 'Turn round and go back!'

And really, that first tank halted. The whole army stood still. Grandfather touched the leading tank with his outstretched fingers, and kept pouring out towards it the same suggestion: 'Turn round and go back, turn round and ... ' And then the lieutenant gave a signal with his pennant, and the tank changed its mind and moved forward, but Grandfather never budged, and the tank ran over him and crushed his head, and after that there was nothing standing in the way of the German army.

Afterwards Dad went out to look for Grandfather's head. That leading tank was standing motionless outside Prague, waiting for a crane to come and release it, because Grandfather's head was mashed between the tracks. And the tracks being turned just the way they were, Dad begged to be allowed to free Grandfather's head and bury it with his body, as was only right for a Christian.

After that there were arguments raging about it all round our district. Some were shouting that Grandfather was a fool, but others retorted that he wasn't quite such a fool, for if everybody'd taken a stand against the Germans like Grandfather, they said, only with weapons in their hands, who could say how it would have turned out for the Germans?

At that time we were still living outside the town, it was only afterwards that we moved into it, and I, who had always been accustomed to solitude, felt the whole world close in on me as soon as we entered the town. The only times I've been able to breathe freely, ever since, were when I was able to get out of it. And again, as soon as I came back, as soon as the streets and alleys shrank in on me as I crossed the bridge, I shrank, too. I always had the impression — and I still have and always shall have — that behind every window there was at the very least one pair of eyes watching me. If anyone spoke to me I blushed, because I felt uncomfortably aware that there was something about me that disturbed and upset everybody. Three months ago I slashed my wrists, and on the face of it I had no reason to do such a thing, but I did have a reason, and I knew what it was, and I was only afraid that everyone who looked at me was guessing at what that reason could be. Hence these eyes behind every window.

What should a young fellow like me have preying on his mind, at only twenty-two years of age? Well, what I had preying on my mind was that the people in our town were staring at me like this because they were convinced I'd cut my veins, that time, simply to get out of working, leaving them to do my share as well as their own, just as they'd had to do for Great-grandfather Luke, and Grandfather Vilém the hypnotist, and for my dad, who had only gone running up and down on locomotives for a quarter of a century so that he could do nothing for ever after.

This year the Germans had lost control of the airspace over our little town. When I rode along the footpath to the fuselage of the aircraft the snow was glittering on the level fields, and in every crystal of snow there seemed to be an infinitely tiny second hand ticking, the snow crackled so in the brilliant sunlight, shimmering in many colours. Then it seemed to me that I could hear these tiny hands ticking away not only in every crystal of snow, but somewhere else as well. There was the ticking of my watch, of course, I heard that quite distinctly, but I could hear another ticking, too, and this one came from the aeroplane, from this heap of wreckage in front of me.

And there it was, the clock on the instrument panel, actually still going, and it even showed the exact time, I compared it with the hands of my watch. And then I saw something else, there underneath the wreck, a glove lit up by the sun, and I realized that this glove wasn't on its own there, but had a human hand inside it, and that this human hand wasn't alone, but was attached to an arm, and the arm to a human body which lay somewhere under the wreckage.

I tramped on the pedals of my bicycle with all the weight of my body. The miniature second hands ticked on every side, crackling in the sunlight, and along the railway track in the distance hurtled a goods train, also crackling merrily. It was the coal train on its way back to the Most coalfield, a hundred and forty axles for sure, and in the middle of the train there was a brake-block that had jammed, and it was red-hot, and metal was dripping on to the track, but that German locomotive bowled gaily along, hauling this jammed wagon just like all the rest.

Tomorrow I'm going back on duty. Again I shall stand by the double track in my little station, where all the trains running from west to east are signalized by odd numbers, according to the schedule, and all the trains from west to east by even numbers. After a break of three months I shall be controlling traffic again, responsible for a station with two main lines passing through it, the through line from west to east bearing the number one, and the other through line from east to west the number two. Then, counting from line number one, all the lines on the right have odd numbers, three, five, seven, and so on, and all the lines on the right from through line number two have even numbers, four, six, eight, ten, and so on.

Of course, that numbering is only for us state railways employees. From the point of view of a layman standing on a railway platform, as it might be in my station, the first line is the fifth, the second is the third, the third line is the first, and the fourth is the second ...

So early tomorrow morning I shall put on my uniform, black trousers and blue tunic, and my service greatcoat with the brass buttons that Mum cleans for me with Sidol. I shall button up that beautiful collar, bearing on both jacket and greatcoat the same insignia, from which every railwayman can see at a glance my status in the service. The central-school button on my collar tells everyone that I've passed my maturity, and the splendid star next to it, embroidered in gold thread, signifies that I'm a traffic apprentice. And then comes the finest symbol of all, here on my collar, the winged wheel decorated with violet and blue spangles, a winged wheel like a little golden sea-horse.

That's how I shall set out in the morning, while it's still dark; and my mother will gaze after me, standing quite still behind the curtains. And in just the same way there'll be people standing behind all the windows, wherever I pass, and like my mother they'll watch me, with a finger parting the curtains. And I shall ride along to the river, where I shall halt for a breath of air on the footpath, as I always do, because I don't like going to work by train. Along by the river I can breathe freely. There are no windows there, no trap waiting for me, no needle jabbed from behind into the nape of my neck.

IN the traffic office everything was just as it had been when I left it. The block-system that controlled the closures of the lines always looked like a mammoth barrel-organ, or a Forbes fruit-machine. The telegraph table stood beneath a window from which you could see five kilometres of a long field road bordered with old apple trees, and at the end of the road glittered Prince Kinský's castle, which I'd seen this morning at sunrise standing one storey deep in mist, so that it appeared to be hanging from a golden chain. On this table under the window there were three telegraph instruments, manufactured half a century ago by the firm of Siemens Halske, and three telegraph diaries. Our two track telephones and the three station telephones were always connected all day long, and the traffic office was always vibrating to the gentle humming and jingling and twittering of telegraphs and telephones, like the shop of some dealer in singing birds. Across the small window into the waiting-room we always had a green curtain hanging from brass rings, and right beside it stood an iron cupboard, and the machine for dating tickets.

Dispatcher Hubička welcomed me back, and told me at once that we were to be on duty together, for after three months off sick I should have to start learning all over again. And then he asked me what the time was, and pulled up my sleeve from my wrist, but instead of looking at my watch he was

11

staring straight at the scar over my healed wound.

I blushed scarlet and turned away quickly, pretending that I was searching for my red cap. I found it in the cupboard; it was covered with dust, and mice had left the tiny prints of their paws across the crown. In the early-morning sun I brushed my uniform cap, and listened to the station-master's pigeons cooing in the pigeon-loft.

Just outside the station premises there was a field where all the jumps for a race-track were laid out, a complete miniature of the course for the Pardubice Grand Steeplechase, because Prince Kinský used to breed half-pure-blood racehorses, which in their time had won him not only the Grand Pardubice but even the Grand National, almost a million pounds sterling. That was so much money in those days that the Prince began to build a gigantic cinema and theatre and concert-hall for our village, just behind our little station, but he never finished it. Instead he turned it into a warehouse for grain, the most magnificent grain-store in the world; even the entrance was through a portico of Roman and Greek columns. And this grain warehouse was known by the English name of Liverpool.

Precisely at half past seven the station-master came into the traffic office. He weighed almost sixteen stone, but women always said that he was incredibly light on his feet when he danced. He combed his hair carefully so as to smooth it from the left side over his bald patch to the right side, and again from his right ear over the bald patch to the left side. But sometimes when he walked out on to the open platform without due care, and there was a wind blowing, it blew the strands apart, and stood both wings of his hair on end like a Gothic arch.

Now he was just opening the door that led to his

own office. No one would ever have expected the station-master of such a tiny station to have an office furnished like this. The Persian carpet glowed with red and blue flowers, and three Turkish stools heightened the oriental effect. The broad leaves of a large palm tree curtained his heavy working table, inlaid with mahogany, and formed a kind of royal umbrella above his Venetian armchair. In fact the whole office left you with the feeling that it ought to be carried round on a palanquin, complete with the station-master in it, as they carry the Pope. On a rococo cabinet stood a marble clock, and instead of a pendulum it had three little gilded balls, revolving first this way and then that, and everybody who ever heard that clock strike, every single one, always turned to look at it and said: What a beautiful chime that clock has! The official service couch, upholstered in chocolate-brown oilcloth, also stood in this office, and on the wall hung a big oil painting, portraying an express locomotive just setting out from Wilson Station, pouring out steam along the track and into the sky, and moving off in a cloud, a picture which was deeply moving to every state railways employee, including our station-master, who had two lifelong ambitions, to be promoted to Inspector of State Railways, and to achieve the title: Baron Lánský of the Rose; because he'd discovered, when he was hunting up his ancestors, that he had a few drops of blue blood in his veins. So he had a double claim to blue blood, because people call us railwaymen the blue aristocracy.

But aside from this preoccupation of his, our station-master took delight in a quite ordinary plebeian hobby, and that was breeding pigeons. Before the war he used to keep Nurembergs, the kind with the aggressive black and white arrowheads on their wings, and he himself used to clean out their loft, and change their water and scatter their feed-corn every other day. But when the Germans made such a savage attack on the Poles, and crushed them in such a barbarous way, our station-master left the flight-hatch of the loft closed one day, and went away to Hradec, but before he left he gave his assistant orders to wring the necks of all those Nurembergs. And after a week he came back from Hradec with some Polish silver-points, those birds with the lovely blue crop and the beautiful wings, ornamented with grey and white triangles bonded into each other like floor-tiles in a bathroom.

I was standing between the tracks when I felt that someone was watching me, and when I turned round I met the eyes of the station-master's wife through the open window of the cellar. She was there in the darkness, feeding her gander and staring at me. I was fond of Mrs Lánská, she liked to come and sit in the office with us in the evenings. She was crocheting a big table-cover, and such a quietness seemed to grow out of this crocheting of hers. More flowers and more birds kept appearing beneath her fingers every minute, and on the telegraph table in front of her she kept a kind of little book, and leaned over it every now and again to pick up the next instructions on manipulating her thread, as though she was playing the guitar and reading from the music.

And yet regularly every Friday Mrs Lánská killed rabbits. She'd take a rabbit from the hutch, clap him between her legs, and then she stuck a blunt knife into his neck and cut with it, and the poor little beast would squeal and whistle for a long time, until after a while his squealing grew weaker and died away. But all the time the station-master's wife would look exactly the same as when she was crocheting her big table-cover. She said that in this way, when the rabbit bled to death, his meat was much tastier and tenderer. Right now I could see her in advance, finishing off this gander she was fattening. She'd straddle him like a horse, clap his orange bill tight against his throat, just like shutting a penknife, and then first she'd carefully pluck out the top feathers, and then his blood would run out into a casserole, and the bird would grow feebler and feebler until he turned quite limp and collapsed under her, and Mrs Lánská would be left sitting only on her own heels.

'Apprentice Hrma!' the station-master called across to me.

I went into the office, saluted, and drew myself to my full height.

'Apprentice Miloš Hrma reporting for duty, sir!'

'Sit down,' he invited me, and as he rose from his table a leaf of the palm laid itself on his head. He stood before me for a moment, his watery eyes wandering over my uniform, and then he did up a button on my tunic for me. 'Well, Hrma, I don't know whether you've noticed that we haven't got our young lady telegraphist here?'

'Virginia Svatá!' I exclaimed.

'Virginia ... Hah!' exploded the station-master. 'Do you mean to tell me you haven't heard anything about it in the town?'

'No, sir, I haven't. Why, whatever can have happened?'

'That's queer! It's a marvel they aren't running mass excursions to our distinguished dispatcher by this time! As though he had four legs! Two heads! A fine way he's found of bringing our quiet, well-conducted station into the limelight, a fine way!'

15

'Oh, if it's Mr Hubička, yes, of course, that's another matter,' I said. 'When I was serving in Dobrovice and Mr Hubička was teaching me, why, yes, the whole line was coming in to have a look at him then, too ... That was the time when he and a certain lady tore the station-master's couch ... '

'What, an Austrian oilcloth couch?' Mr Lánský's eyes bulged. 'Like this one of mine?'

'Yes, just like that one,' I said.

'Sit down, Miloš,' exhorted the station-master, growing very affable. And he himself sat down astride a second stool, and laid a hand expectantly behind his ear.

'It was after the last passenger train of the evening had left,' I confided into Mr Lánský's ear. 'All the evening we'd had this very fancy lady sitting with us in the traffic office, smoking cigarettes and drinking wine. And towards midnight Dispatcher Hubička said to me : Miloš, you're only just out of school, but I trust you. Take over for me, just for a couple of hours. And so I stayed on duty, and Mr Hubička took this lady away into the station-master's office. And every now and again I put my ear to the door of the station-master's office, and I could hear : 'Kitten, the body needs it, the body cries out for it ... '

'That swinish, hairy, rooting pig!' hooted the station-master, and hoisted himself up to stare through the window, past the bowing and cooing pigeons, to the platform, where the dispatcher was standing.

'If only it was there to be seen on him, at least, that scoundrelly nature of his!' yelled Mr Lánský; and Mr Hubička thrust the tip of a finger into his ear and shook it, as though he had some water singing in his ear.

'Still waters run deep,' I said. 'But about an hour

after midnight, when the freight engine had taken the wagons of sugar away, I listened, and I heard from inside the station-master's office such a queer noise, like shoving a coffin along ... And then ... crash! I rushed into the station-master's office, and there was that lady lying on the couch on her back, naked, with her legs spread out like this! And Dispatcher Hubička was sprawling on the floor in his underpants, just like the soldier in the picture in our church, when the sepulchre burst open. And he says to me: Miloš, I badly miscalculated the counter-spin. I've fallen from the altar of love ... '

'The spotted hyena!' shrieked Mr Lánský, and leaned on the frame of the window and glared at the dispatcher, who stood with legs spread at ease on the platform, gazing at the sky.

'And how did you say that hussy was lying on the station-master's couch?' demanded Mr Lánský, turning back to me. 'Tell me again about that!'

'I'll show you,' I said, pointing to the identical oilcloth couch, 'if you'll allow me.' And I flung myself down on it, turning in mid-air so that I dropped flat on my back. The station-master leaned over me, petrified with horror.

'Let him wallow like that with his strumpets in the waiting-room! But not on his station-master's couch!'

'Of course not!' I said. 'Nobody should sit on the station-master's couch except the station-master himself.'

'You see! *You* realize that for yourself, but to that swinish pig nothing is sacred!' he cried.

I sat up again and went on: 'But, sir, that still isn't all. Look!' And I took Mr Lánský by the sleeve and pointed: 'And here — right *here* and *here* — the oilcloth was ripped right across ...'

'They'd torn the couch!' wailed the station-master. 'Ripped the station-master's couch in half! That is what comes of it when there's nothing above folks any more! Neither God nor myth, neither allegory nor symbol ... We're on our own in this world, so everything's allowed. But not for me! For me there is a God! But for that grunting pig nothing exists but pork, dumplings and cabbage ... '

And the station-master said no more, but only fumed and snorted, staring out on to the platform, at Dispatcher Hubička's back.

'It's the devil!' he said after a while. 'A fellow who could have been a station-master a good ten years ago, somewhere at some bit of a halt on a single-track line, and he still hasn't got so much as a single star. As fast as they consider promoting him, he comes up with some swinishness, while I move steadily up the ladder.'

'I've heard', I said, 'that you're going to be promoted to Inspector of State Railways.'

'Yes, so I am.'

'Ah, and then', I cried, 'instead of three small stars you'll have just one, but bordered with the inspector's field!'

'That's right, Miloš,' said Mr Lánský dreamily. 'That's the kind of example you have here,' he said, and opened his cupboard and drew out a new tunic, with the field with the diamond star already stitched on to it. 'That's the kind of example you have in me, and here am I casting my pearls before swine.'

'An inspector, like that,' I said, 'that's the same rank on the railways as a major in the army, isn't it?'

'That's right, Miloš,' said Mr Lánský.

A long goods train rushed by on line number one, going at full speed, and the axles running over the joins in the rails gave out deep, regular, throbbing sounds. The station-master carefully folded away the sleeves and edges of his new tunic in the cupboard, so that he could close the door properly. Then he picked up the box of feed-corn, and opened the window, and the Polish silver-points flew into the office, fighting in mid-air for the privilege of sitting on his shoulders. They perched all over him, like on a monument or a fountain, bowing and fawning on him, but they didn't care at all about the corn, it was love that mattered more to them. They pecked at his cheeks, but so tenderly, as though they'd been his little children.

The goods train carried its racket away with it. That roar and rush of a train in motion is something that goes on always the same, just as in time of peace every evening train scatters squares and oblongs of light from its glowing windows.

'But what can Mr Hubička have been getting up to with Virginia, then?' I asked.

'Bestiality,' said Mr Lánský, smiling and offering his lips to the pigeons, 'except that a beast wouldn't get mixed up in such goings-on. But I'm not going to get worked up about this any more, Miloš, the disciplinary committee in Hradec is in charge of it now ... Not to make a long story of it, they were on night duty together, and Dispatcher Hubička bowled Virginia over, and then turned up her skirt and printed all our station stamps, one after another, all over our telegraphist's backside. Even the date-stamp he stuck on her there! But in the morning, when Virginia got home, her mother read all those stamps printed on her, and came running here immediately, threatening to complain to the Gestapo! I had to write a protocol, Miloš. Terrible! And Virginia had to go at once to headquarters, and there the Director of State Railways himself examined all those stamps — in person! Dreadful!' cried the station-master, and the pigeons fell lurching from his outstretched arms, and beat wildly with their wings to keep their balance. Along the station fence, there on the opposite side of the lines, a black stallion came galloping with the Countess Kinská on his back, just coming back from the farms. She galloped as though she'd grown as part of that black stallion. Mr Lánský went out on to the platform with his Polish silver-points, and bowed to the galloping Countess Kinská, who was crossing the track and pulling up her mount at the entrance to the station. She slid down very lightly from her horse, except that her riding-breeches clung to the leather saddle; and then the station-master kissed her hand and strolled up and down with her, wreathed in Polish silver-points, and the Countess, as though this was perfectly understandable and taken for granted, showed no surprise or wonder at all at these pigeons, but held out her gloved hand to them, and went on conversing with the station-master.

Dispatcher Hubička was free to let his eyes dwell on the Countess.

'Miloš, you know what I wish? I wish I could be that saddle,' and he pointed to the saddled black stallion, and then spat and laughed, and said to me confidentially: 'Miloš, I had a beautiful dream. I dreamed I was changed into a cart, and the Countess held me by the shafts and steered herself and me into the warehouse.' And again he looked so lewdly at the Countess, eyeing her legs as she walked along with Mr Lánský towards the grain-store called Liverpool.

The station-master seemed to be so horrified, presumably by something the Countess had just been saying to him, that all the pigeons took flight in alarm from his shoulders, and flew away. And then the Countess held out her hand to him, and he kissed it reverently, and wanted to help her into her stirrups, but the Countess restrained him with a wave of her hand, and vaulted on to the black stallion, opening her legs wide for an instant. And Mr Hubička wiped his mouth, and declared:

'There's a smashing bummie!' and spat.

The Countess galloped away along the road from the station, the black stallion bounding high from the snow, which glittered now in rosy sunlight. Mr Hubička divided women into two categories. Those who carried their most striking attributes below the waist he called by the name he'd just applied to the Countess: bummies. And those who had beautiful and notable bosoms he called: busters. Just as you might use the terms curlie, smiler, blondie, and so on.

Mr Lánský bore down on the station doorway in a rage, hissing at us:

'You see, Hubička, even Countess Kinská has already heard about your goings-on!'

And he turned about in the doorway, wagging his head with terrible gravity, and charged straight up the stairs into the kitchen, where he began by banging a chair violently on the floor several times, until flakes of plaster fell from the ceiling in the traffic office below; and then he hallooed into the ventilating shaft:

'The curse of this erotic century! Everything's saturated with sex, nothing but sex and erotic stimulants! Adolescents and even children fall in love with goose-girls! Love tragedies are common currency, all through reading sexy books and watching erotic films! To the courts with these writers and educators, these purveyors of pornography! Away with the monstrous imaginings of these young folks! That fellow cutting up the milk-woman's corpse ... and he'd have cut up his own cousin's corpse, too, if he hadn't been prevented. Drug-stores flaunting cut-outs of young women, side view, *in section, life-size* ... and the young people just gulp it down wholesale. There's one artist's studio would make you wonder if you hadn't strayed into a butcher's shop dealing in human meat. Cannibalism! This woman Vranská in a trunk, and now they're looking for a fair man with a gold tooth. Bought her an Australian apple for the last time, in the Crown automat. Ugh! Just butchers' meat! Murders for lechery from here to the horizon! Into the dock with these teachers who allow sex education! The more immorality and hedonism, the less cradles and the more coffins!' rasped the station-master through the ventilating shaft, from the kitchen on the first floor down into the traffic office.

This was all because, for one thing, Mr Lánský was a member of the S.P.R., the Society for Public Regeneration, in Prague, and then also the Countess, when she came to order the wagons for the fattened cattle, often reproached him with being lukewarm in the faith, saying that when the Catholic church fell the whole world would fall. So whenever Mr Lánský passed by a church, if he was in uniform he saluted it, or if he was in civilian clothes he took off his Schwarzenberg hat and bowed to the church, and at the same time mumbled something in a quiet, conversational tone.

THE block-system rattled, a red circle there jerked and changed to white, and I pulled out the key from the board and ran out on to the platform, into the alcove where the signal levers were. A locomotive was whistling at the approach to the station, and the station-master came down the stairs again, just as though nothing had happened; he seemed to be somehow purged clean by that yelling into the ventilator shaft, as though he used it as a wailing wall. Hubička used to say that he was in the habit of shouting at his wife in just the same way, and she — though she was the daughter of a butcher from Volary — put up with it most of the time, but about four times a year she'd stage a rebellion, and when Mr Lánský was just in full cry with his yelling at her and laying down for her what a decent woman ought to be, his wife would heave at him whatever happened to come to hand. Once, before Christmas, when he was shouting at her like this, she dragged him into the bathroom and gave him such a clout that he went souse into the bath to join the Christmas carp.

Mr Lánský came into the office, and one glance was enough to show him that all was not in order with our traffic.

'What's up, boys?' he said paternally. 'Got a situation on your hands?'

'There was a soldier standing by our demarcation pole there,' said Hubička with a wry grimace.

23

'That close-surveillance transport?' asked the station-master, his eyes popping.

'The one with the three exclamation marks,' I said.

'Have you read ... ?' He pointed to the proclamation signed by the Reich plenipotentiary.

'We've read it,' said Hubička.

'And have you considered ... ?'

'Considered and decided,' said Dispatcher Hubička, and laughed.

'But, boys, this could very well qualify as sabotage,' nodded the station-master, and went out on to the platform.

In the locomotive of the close-surveillance military transport, very pale, was Engineer Honzík, head of the regional *betriebsamt*, who had gone all the way to Liboch himself to escort this train. And now he stood there as a hostage, staring from blank, shocked eyes and wringing his hands; pressed close against the little window of the cab, he demonstrated into the windows and doors of our buildings how our station had been responsible for making a prisoner of him.

Mr Lánský saluted, and I went to the track and saluted, too. The locomotive stopped, and out of it dropped two slender S.S. men, with Parabellum pistols in their fingers, and for a moment they stared at my red cap. I clicked my heels and saluted again, but they fell in one on either side of me, and prodded with the muzzles of their automatic pistols just at the base of my lungs, and I was forced to clamber up the steps to the footplate, and the train began to move. And it seemed strange to me that both these S.S. men were beautiful; to look at them you'd have thought they ought to be writing poetry, or going to play tennis, but there they stood on either side of me in the locomotive, and beside Engineer Honzík

24

stood the commander of this transport, a captain in an Austrian mountain cap, and across his face he had a healed scar that jumped clean across his mouth and continued on down his chin; even the engine-driver was in uniform; he was holding the regulator handle and sitting in an upholstered armchair, it was a German engine burning black coal, and beside the driver's seat there was a lever like the one you see on an invalid's chair, so that the seat can be transformed into a reclining bed. And those two S.S. men all the time kept the muzzles of their pistols jammed against the tips of my lungs, and their eyes, just like the muzzles of their guns, stayed fixed, motionlessly watching the captain, but the captain was gazing out over the landscape.

I saw that someone at the farm, out of curiosity, had opened the trap-door and crept out on to the tin roof, and now he was raising his arms, as if in surrender. They'd surely shouted at him from the transport, and no doubt they were aiming a gun at him, and the man on the roof had his hands lifted high, just like when he drank to the sun. It was our village idiot, Jordan, who took the cows to pasture, and whiled away the time on summer Sunday afternoons by tucking a bottle of beer into a little fishing net and going for a row in a boat, and every now and again he'd pull out his fishing net and pour some fresh beer into his glass, and then he'd stand up in the boat, like he was standing now on the roof, he'd stand up in the boat in his track-suit, and with his hand lifted high he'd drink to the sun. First he'd call out to it, let out a yell of: Hey, hey, hey! and then he'd drink the beer off to the bottom. I saw the station-master's wife, too, behind the kitchen window; her eyes were separated by the brass rail on which the little curtains hung, she raised her hands, and the next moment the locomotive of the close-surveillance transport was running alongside the shot-up train on line number five. I swivelled my eyes round to see what these two would say to that, and they were staring back at me as though it was I who had shot up the train.

'*Du Arschlecker!*' grated the first S.S. man through his teeth.

'Better to shoot such a swine out of hand,' said the second.

'Thirty minutes' delay!' hissed the first, and jabbed the muzzle of his automatic still harder between my ribs.

How different it had been when I set out that other time, three months ago, in search of my death. I leaned down to the cash-desk — it was in the evening, and the booking-clerk had red hair — I said : One single, please! And she recognized me, and said : Oh, but, Mr Hrma, where to? I said : I'll go wherever your eye first happens to light. And she giggled : What do you mean, first happens to light! I spend my life looking at these tickets. I said : You know what, miss? You look at me, and with your left hand pull out a ticket. And she laughed : But, Mr Hrma, I could sell these tickets even in the dark. She was laughing because she thought I was joking. And then I said : All right, the seventh column, the seventh drawer, lucky seven, same as for the Jews. And she reached her hand there, and all the time she was looking at me, she never took her eyes from me, and she said : It'll be to Bystřice by Benešov, and it'll cost you umpteen crowns ...

The engine shook, the planes of snow receded, gleaming, into the distance, thawing snow, ticking away steadily with all its prismatic crystals. In a ditch lay three dead horses, just as the Germans had thrown them out of the wagons in the night. They simply opened the doors and threw out the corpses. Now they lay in the ditch beside the permanent way, legs stretched stiffly towards the sky like columns on which depended the invisible portal of heaven. Engineer Honzík looked at me, and his eyes were full of grief and anger because it was in his section that this close-surveillance transport had been delayed. And it was certainly I who was to blame, so it was only justice that these S.S. men had forced me aboard the engine, and were all the time waiting and wanting to be allowed to place the muzzles of their pistols to the nape of my neck, give the signal, press the trigger and dispatch the bullets into me, and then open the little door ...

This I felt quite clearly and precisely, and yet I thought it must be nonsense, after all, just a show, that they were not capable of it, because they were so handsome and dandified. I always had a horror of beautiful people, I've never been able to talk coherently to them, I always sweated and stammered, I had such an admiration for beauty, and was so dazzled by it, that I never could look a handsome person in the face.

But the captain, on the other hand, was ugly, what with that long scar carved across his face, as though he'd fallen with his face on a sharp pot when he was young, and this captain was now looking at me. I put up my hand to hang on to a kind of tab that swung from the roof of the engine. I ventured to do this because the captain had his eyes fixed on me absently, and he saw that I was just the simpleton whose job it was to stand by the line, the simpleton who'd been put here by the directorate in Hradec Králové to stand by the line and lower and raise the signals, while the German army first swept through his station towards the east, and now trailed back again. I said to myself: All the same, the Germans are fools. Dangerous fools. I'd been a bit of a fool myself, too, but to my own hurt, while with the Germans it was always to the hurt of someone else.

They were standing on line number five once, a whole train-load of soldiers, and they went off to buy foodstuffs and sugar and cubes of synthetic honey at the shop in the village, until one soldier stealthily drew out the cube on which the others were standing, and the synthetic honey all fell down, and the shopkeeper counted the cubes, and found that five were missing; and the train commandant ordered the whole company to entrain, and right up to the evening he was searching the entire train, hunting for those cubes of synthetic honey, and when he failed to find them he went in person to the shopkeeper, and saluted, and ceremoniously apologized to him ... And maybe these were those very Germans, standing with me now in the locomotive, maybe the very same.

The fireman winked at me merrily, and then fanned away with his shovel at the coal; first he tossed some well on to the back of his fire, and then into the middle, with rhythmic movements, so that with the last shovelful he was deploying the coal at the very edge of the firebox. And the captain's eyes were gazing now at my wrist, where I, too, had a scar; my sleeve had slipped down, and the captain looked at that healed wound like a man reading a book. Perhaps this captain had already learned much more, perhaps he was looking at everything now from the opposite viewpoint, and his eyes were like two fragments of stone. And now they were all staring at my wrist, and the captain stretched out his little whip, and with it drew back my other sleeve, too, and looked at the second scar.

'*Kamerad*,' he said.

And he made a sign, and the close-surveillance military transport slowed down, and the two pistols were withdrawn from my back, and then I wasn't looking at those two handsome soldiers any more, but only gazing at the footplate under me, the grooved iron plating that was constantly moving as the locomotive crept slowly along the rails.

'Go,' said the captain.

'Thank you,' I whispered.

And all the time I didn't know whether this was a joke or not. I opened the little door and stepped down on to the first step, and then with every step lower and lower, until I stretched out one foot and dropped on to the walk alongside the track, like somebody doing a Cossack dance, then one more jump, and I was standing still, and the locomotive set off again, gathering speed, and alongside me flowed the open vans with the Tigers. Some of the soldiers had kilo cans of preserves opened, and their sleeves rolled up, and were stabbing pieces of meat with their knives, and eating; others, with their automatic guns across their knees, were swinging their jackboots as if they were dabbling their feet in a brook. As each of those wagons passed me I had the feeling all the time that my back might still make a good target.

The last wagon of this transport was a box-car, open, and I saw women's black stockings swinging from it, maybe nurses from a field hospital; but until that moment I'd been within range of German pistols, revolvers and automatics, for with Germans, as I'd confirmed now in my own skin, nobody can ever be sure what they will do. Mrs Karásková, who lives right next door to us, was imprisoned by the Germans as early as nineteen forty, and she came back last year at Christmas, and the whole of that time, the whole four years, she'd been in Gestapo headquarters at Pečkárna, and there she mopped up the blood after executions, all those four years she spent mopping up blood, and the chief executioner was kind to her; he used to give her ham, and ask her to sing for him: Why do you weep, black eyes? and he always said: Please! to her, and: I beg your pardon. And then out of the blue they suddenly sent her home, for good, and wrote her a letter of apology into the bargain; but Mrs Karásková had gone out of her wits with all this. At the Labour Office they found her a place in the engine-sheds, they put an oil-can in her hand, and she had to fill up and wipe the bearings of the machines.

I was drawing near to the curve of the track; already the twelve hooves of those dead horses were visible in the distance, jutting towards the sky like the columns in the cathedral crypt at Stará Boleslav. I thought of Masha, and of how we met for the first time, when I was still with the track superintendent. He gave us two buckets of red paint and told us to paint the fence round the entire state workshops. Masha began by the railway track, just as I did. We stood facing each other with the tall wire fence between us, at our feet we each had a bucket of cinnabar paint, we each had a brush, and we stippled away with our brushes opposite each other and painted that fence, she from her side and I from mine.

There were four kilometres altogether of this fence; for five months we stood facing each other like this, and there wasn't anything we didn't say to each other, Masha and I, but always there was

this fence between us. After we'd painted two kilometres of it, one day I'd done just as high as Masha's
mouth with this red colour, and I told her that I
loved her, and she, from her side, had painted just up
to there, too, and she said that she loved me, too ...
and she looked into my eyes, and, as this was in a
ditch and among tall goosefoot plants, I put out my
lips, and we kissed through the newly painted fence,
and when we opened our eyes she had a sort of tiny
red fence-pale striped across her mouth, and so had
I, and we burst out laughing, and from that moment
on we were happy.

When I came to those dead horses, I sat down on
the belly of one of them, and leaned my head against
his leg. The head of the second horse was gazing at
me with bulging eyes, as though even this dead horse
had lived with me through what might very well
have happened to me only a few minutes ago.

I went up the stairs of the little hotel, that time
in Bystřice by Benešov, and at the turn of the stairs
there was a bricklayer at work, in white clothes; he
was chiselling channels in the wall to cement in two
hooks, on which in a little while he was going to
hang a Minimax fire-extinguisher; and this bricklayer was already an old man, but he had such an
enormous back that he had to turn round to let me
pass by, and then I heard him whistling the waltz
from *The Count of Luxembourg* as I went into my
little room. It was afternoon. I took out two razors,
and one of them I scored blade-up into the top of
the bathroom stool, and the other I laid beside it,
and I, too, began to whistle the waltz from *The Count
of Luxembourg* while I undressed and turned on the
hot-water tap, and then I reflected, and very quietly
I opened the door a crack. And the bricklayer was
standing there in the corridor on the other side of

the door, and it was as if he also had opened the door a crack to have a look at me and see what I was doing, just as I had wanted to have a look at him.

And I slammed the door shut and crept into the bath, I had to let myself down into it gradually, the water was so hot; I gasped with the sting of it as carefully and painfully I sat down. And then I stretched out my wrist, and with my right hand I slashed my left wrist ... and then with all my strength I brought down the wrist of my right hand on the upturned blade I'd grooved into the stool for that purpose. And I plunged both hands into the hot water, and watched the blood flow slowly out of me, and the water grow rosy, and yet all the time the pattern of the red blood flowing remained so clearly perceptible, as though someone was drawing out from my wrists a long, feathery red bandage, a filmy, dancing veil ... and presently I thickened there in the bath, as that red paint thickened when we were painting the fence all round the state workshops, until we had to thin it with turpentine — and my head sagged, and into my mouth flowed pink raspberryade, except that it tasted slightly salty ... and then those concentric circles in blue and violet, trailing feathery fronds like coloured spirals in motion ... and then there was a shadow stooping over me, and my face was brushed lightly by a chin overgrown with stubble. It was that bricklayer in the white clothes. He hoisted me out and landed me like a red fish with delicate red fins sprouting from its wrists. I laid my head on his smock, and I heard the hissing of lime as my wet face slaked it, and that smell was the last thing of which I was conscious.

I sat there on the dead horse, with my head leaning against its erected leg, which jutted towards the sky, and I fingered the little manes that horses have round their hooves ... and a goods train rolled past on the line, whistling merrily. The wagons veiled and unveiled me in a steady rhythm, and I began to shake, and the saliva gushed in my mouth, because the beginning of all this was at Uncle Noneman's, in Karlín, in Prague. I was sleeping there at Masha's uncle's place; they put me up in the studio on a couch, and covered me with a blanket, and then on top of that with the cloth on which was a painting of Prague, with an aeroplane flying above it, in which customers used to have themselves photographed as pilots and observers; whole groups of people used to get into the photograph in this aeroplane, for a lark. Then, in the night, when it was all quiet at the Nonemans', Masha came and crept in under this cloth with the aeroplane, and stroked me and pressed herself against me. And I caressed her, too, and I was man enough until it came to the point of being a man, but then all at once I wilted, and it was all up with everything. Masha tried pinching me, but I'd gone quite dead, as though I were paralysed in all my extremities ... and after an hour Masha crept out again from under the cloth, and went away into the little room, to her aunt ...

And in the morning I couldn't even look at her, I sat completely crushed. Customers started coming, and they stood behind that cloth beneath which I'd gone through such an awful experience in the night. One of them would get up on a chair, and another on a step-ladder, and Uncle Noneman would give each of them a bottle or a funnel to hold, and then he'd creep under the cloth that shrouded his camera, and raise his hand and give them the signal, like someone conducting music, and then duck out again from under the cloth, and after five minutes he brought the photograph, because he had a large

notice over the doorway: FINISHED IN FIVE MINUTES.
They kept coming all the morning, until two German soldiers came, and just when one of them had climbed on the chair and the other on the step-ladder, and Mr Noneman had arranged the cloth with the aeroplane and the panorama of Prague in front of them, there was a thunderous crash, and a great wind surged through the studio and swept away the cloth with the aeroplane, and those two soldiers fell down, and Uncle Noneman, who was just burrowing under his cloth, fell down, too, but that was the least of it. A moment later came a tremendous gust of wind, and I saw the whole wall of the studio roll away, and the gust carried off Uncle and those two soldiers, and blew in Auntie and Masha from the other room, and even though they were flying through the air, at the same time they were trying to hold down their skirts, but they couldn't manage it, and their hair was blown fluttering all ways, curtaining the whole of the sky for me, and down we all went, and sailing like tossed balls we dropped slowly on to the grass outside ... and the last thing that wind blew after us was the board on which was the notice: FINISHED IN FIVE MINUTES ...

Along the main street several people went running, then there was a long silence, and then the sirens began to wail, and a number of ambulances passed, and then came a lot of torn and draggled people, laughing and laughing like crazy men; they dropped on their backs on the grass, lay on their backs and shook with laughter ... and only then did this fellow come along, and turn and point in the direction of Vysočany, and say: A terrible raid, folks! And when he looked down at the grass, at that big notice, he repeated with quite another meaning what was written on it: FINISHED IN FIVE MINUTES ...

I DUCKED under the bars, and there was that passenger train standing on line number five. The whole length of this train was shot to pieces, and on the first wagon I read the label: Destination, state workshops: departure station, Krakow. This was how the partisans always thrashed the German transports close behind the fighting line, not a single passenger carriage had glass in the windows, every one of them had been raked with shots, the plate-metal walls were scrawled with the signature of automatic rifles, some torn apart by grenades, others by shells from a small mountain gun or a looted anti-tank mortar. They were the kind of passenger coaches that had been withdrawn from traffic long ago; doors led from both sides into each compartment, and along the whole wall of the coach there was a single long footboard. At almost every door there were dried brown stains of blood.

I looked into one compartment, everywhere it was the same. Shattered glass on the floor, combs, torn-off buttons, some with fabric still attached, a whole sleeve from a military coat, blood-stained pants, a handkerchief once wet with blood, scattered chessmen, a board for the dice game called 'Don't be angry, lad!', a round mirror, a mouth-organ, letters spattered with snow, a long bandage and a child's striped ball. I picked up one letter, decorated with the print of a hobnailed military boot. *Mein Lieber Schnucki Pucki!* the letter began, and ended: *Deine*

Luise. And the print of a girl's lips. In a corner there was an unlaced military boot grinning at me with its tongue lolling out. On the floor lay two dead rooks.

When I came home from the hospital there were such hard frosts that in the little wood just outside our town, where colonies of rooks and crows always gathered, the trees were wreathed with these black birds; they gleamed in the frosty sun of morning, and when I came to the wood I saw thousands of these rooks lying about the ground, round every tree, like over-ripe Bosnian plums … a whole wood full of dead, even those which were still roosting in the branches, even they were dead, frozen in their sleep. I stamped the sole of my shoe against the trunk of a tree, that time, and out of the boughs and branches showered hoar-frost and dead birds; several of them brushed my shoulders, but they were so light that it was only as if an empty beret had fallen on me.

I jumped down from the last footboard of this train on line five, and looked into the office. Dispatcher Hubička had his feet up on the telegraph table, his hands tucked under his armpits, his chin dropped into his chest, and he was asleep.

Well, that was something I was capable of, too; I, too, have fallen asleep on duty when the fit came over me. All of a sudden you get such a longing to drowse that the best thing is to have a nap at the first opportunity that offers. But this sleep that dispatchers indulge in on duty is governed by some special signalling system. The body may be deeply asleep, but something in the dispatcher's head is stirring. It's enough if the telegraph calls, and your proper dispatcher instantly gets up, throws the switch of his instrument, gives the station sign, and sits down again and is instantly fast asleep, but when the report on the white telegraph tape ends, the dispatcher wakes up, gives the received and understood signal, adds the sign of his station with his telegraph key, stops the machine, sits down again, and goes back to sleep. Or again, such a proper dispatcher will set his approach signal and go to sleep, but he'll hear any step that comes near him, and he hears when the locomotive of the approaching train stamps its way on to the isolated section of rail, and in the block-system in the traffic office that's only a light tap, as if somebody had dropped a coffee spoon. And the dispatcher awakes, and goes and bangs over the signal.

The moment the station-master could be heard coming down the stairs, the dispatcher planted his boots on the floor and got up. Mr Lánský came in in his old uniform, he was evidently going to clean out the pigeon-loft again; his trousers were whitened all over with pigeon-droppings, and so were his sleeves.

And then I came into the traffic office.

'Dispatcher Miloš Hrma reporting back on duty!' I said.

In an instant they were shaking me by the hand and slapping me on the back, the station-master with tears in his eyes.

'Miloš, what did I say to you? Didn't I warn you to take great care? I tell you again', he said, and turned and pointed his finger at the signature on the proclamation, 'that Reich Plenipotentiary Danko himself announced in Hradec that he wouldn't hesitate for an instant to have a few Czech dispatchers shot!' and he wagged his head, and one of the pigeons, which was waddling about on the platform, cooed loudly, and down to the door of the traffic office flew the whole flock of Polish silver-points.

Into the station steamed a goods train. Mr Lánský went out on to the platform, and the pigeons took flight after him, and settled all over his shoulders and head. He was forced to stretch out his arms, and the Polish silver-points settled on them, too, as on some statue in a square. And the station-master was pleased to have the train chief and his crew looking at him; even the engine-driver stopped cleaning his hands with cotton-waste to stare at our station-master strolling about and carrying with him this flock of birds, all flapping their wings to maintain their hold.

'Miserable coal they've given us,' said the engine-driver. 'This is the second time we've had to get up steam.'

'Well, mate, what's with you, are you still painting?' asked the dispatcher.

'I am that,' nodded the engine-driver; 'just now I'm painting the sea. Good lord, that station-master of yours ought to be in a circus with those pigeons.'

'Potato-puppet theatre!' said the dispatcher. 'But you've taken up painting seascapes, have you?'

I stood on the platform and looked at the train chief and his crew, and the fireman, and I could see at a glance that they'd halted here only so that they could have a look at our Dispatcher Hubička, and see whether they could detect any sign in his appearance of the tales that were going round about him, how he'd turned up our telegraphist's skirt on night duty, and printed the station stamps all over her behind.

'That's right,' said the engine-driver, still staring with admiring eyes at our dispatcher, 'I'm enlarging a seascape from a picture postcard.'

'And what's wrong with coming out like this and painting from nature?' asked the dispatcher.

'Don't talk to me about nature, in nature everything shifts about too much,' cried the engine-driver,
laughing, and he cast a glance towards the goods
wagons and winked; and then they all burst out
laughing. 'If I painted from nature I should have to
reduce everything, instead of enlarging it. Only
once did I let myself tangle with nature. I borrowed
a stuffed vixen from a school, and arranged her
among the underbrush in a wood, and before I could
even begin to sketch her, up came a couple of dogs
and tore the vixen to pieces! Three hundred crowns!
Don't talk to me about nature!'

But Dispatcher Hubička was gazing into the blue
sky, and now, as I followed his gaze, I, too, could
see what he was seeing there: our telegraphist Virginia stretched out across the entire heaven, and Mr
Hubička gently turning up her skirt, and then taking
one stamp after another, and with long movements
printing those stamps on our telegraphist's behind
... and I saw that the train crew and the engine crew,
all of them were gazing at the sky, and all of them
were seeing the same thing there, that beautiful
incident on account of which they had made this
halt here, under the pretence of raising a head of
steam.

And when they'd done gazing at the sky they gazed
in wonder at Dispatcher Hubička, who was suddenly
transformed into a handsome man. Even those
wrinkles round his mouth, even his slightly bandy
legs became him. I grasped that for women our dispatcher had an assured enchantment.

'You know how I'm painting the sea from that
picture postcard?' asked the engine-driver. 'This
board I'm painting on, I fasten it in my vice. Then
I pin the picture postcard to my work-bench, and I
paint. But somehow I seem to be ham-handed. I can

never get that real break of the surf, that sea-swell on to my board, not like it is on the postcard.'

'Mr Kníže,' said Dispatcher Hubička, 'you try fastening the postcard into your vice, too, right beside your board ... and then take your brush, and go over the line of the waves on the postcard with it, like this ... like this, trace over the waves with your brush until you get the feel of it into your hand, and then you make these waves bigger and bigger until they're the size you need, and then slap them straight on to the board.'

'Man, but you've got ideas ... !' marvelled the engine-driver.

I ran into the traffic office, where the telephone was ringing. I could hear the station-master making believe to abuse his Polish silver-points, for all the pigeons were up in the loft with him by this time. Some day I should really like to hide myself in that pigeon-loft and watch through a chink, and see what the station-master gets up to there with his pigeons. I even had the impression that the pigeons were laughing at his scolding, up there, and that in the end he'd grab at some unruly pigeon and smack its bottom ...

I had the bakelite receiver at my ear, and was gazing along the platform, where the men were standing in the sunshine, and just then the engine-driver leaned forward to whisper something to Mr Hubička. But now that I was looking at the coal-trucks like this, sidelong, I got a shock. Out of the wagons jutted the horns of cattle, and several heads reared up and turned their eyes towards the platform, and they were great, cows' eyes, full of curiosity and grief. And in almost every one of those wagons the floor was trampled clean through, and from the hole protruded a cow's foot, bruised, unmoving, turning blue ... oh, this I didn't like, this I couldn't bear! ... When they were transporting hungry calves, and the train stopped at my station, at least I used to offer them my fingers through the door of the box-car, to comfort them with the illusion of the udder, if only for a few moments, but I didn't like it, I didn't! nor those vans full of young kids, when the butchers carried them with their little feet tied with rope so tightly that they were numbed and dead, I couldn't bear it, I couldn't *bear* it! nor when they moved little pigs to the Prague slaughter-houses in open two-decker wagons in the frosts, little pigs with their heads pressed together, afraid to move in case by a single movement they dispelled a little more of what warmth they had, pigs with frozen feet, poor little porcelain trotters! oh, this was something I never could stand! nor when they took them in the hot days of summer, without water, all the way from Hungary, a whole train-load of little pigs with jaws wide open, gaping with thirst, like birds dying of drought ...

I ran out of the traffic office.

'Where did this load come from?' I asked the train chief.

'From the front, ten days those cattle have been on the road,' he said, and waved his hand.

I jumped up on the rim of a wagon and looked down into it. And all those cattle were down with strangles, several of them were lying there dead; from one cow's rump hung a dead and rotting calf ... everywhere nothing but terrible pairs of eyes silently reproaching, tortured eyes over which I wrung my hands. A whole train-load of the reproachful eyes of cattle.

'Those Germans are swine!' I cried.

The train chief waved his hand and called back:

'Swine, that's putting it mildly! Those last three wagons there are full of sheep dying wholesale … they're grazing one another's fleeces from hunger!'

'We've got a head of steam now,' said the engine-driver, and added quietly: 'Have you heard? Last night the partisans near Jihlava blew up one of those close-surveillance transports so neatly that the whole thing dropped into a ravine, and with the second blast they dropped the bridge right on top of the train.'

And he climbed up into his engine and drew back the lever, and the goods train started to move again, and took away those wagons bristling with cows' feet and cows' eyes, wagons with feet stamped clean through their floors and sticking out below, all bruised and soiled with coal-dust, dangling along the sleepers. And behind the Liverpool grain warehouse, alongside the ramp, there were two wagons drawn up, brought in by the mail train in the morning, wagons consigned to the Prague slaughter-houses.

After that two close-surveillance military transports went through, all tanks, all Tigers, each train with a commandant aboard the locomotive, maybe already in consequence of the partisans' work near Jihlava. And from the village the drovers were herding in the beef cattle; if any of the beasts resisted, the herdsmen broke their tails. One cow in her despair lay down in the highway, and the drovers shoved a wisp of straw under her tail and set fire to this straw. Then a cart came driving in from the estate farm, with the horses straining at the traces, because there was a bull tied on behind; he had broken knees, and a torn nose from having ripped the ring out of his nostrils. Now he was tied by his horns to the cart, and dragged along like that. Maybe this bull had realized, too late, that the girl who led him was handing him over to the butchers by treachery, betraying him by the scent of her skirt, to which the bull was accustomed, and after which he would have tramped along to the end of the world. Now the cart hauled him along skidding through the thawing snow, and his bloody knees left behind him two red streaks.

'Miloš,' said Mr Hubička, turning to me and taking me by the chin, 'that affair with that S.S. machine ... I'll never forget that. You took that in my place.'

And then the telephone rang from the signal-box.

'The Germans are swine,' I said.

I picked up the telephone, and went stiff with shock.

'Mr Hubička, our signal arm's fallen down!'

'Who did we give the clear to?' he asked.

'The express mail.'

'This is crazy!' he said.

'Mr Hubička,' I said, 'I'll ride over there on my bike and hold up the arm into the clear position.'

And I ran out and rode along the footway past Liverpool to the mast of the signal, climbed up by the hooks, sat astride the lamp and raised the arm of the signal; and the express locomotive of the train was already approaching, the through mail that took the front line food and drink for the officers, as well as letters, passing non-stop through all stations, and yielding precedence only to the close-surveillance military transports. The engine-driver started to slow up in a hurry when he saw me on the signal, but I pulled out my service torch, and with the green light gave him the sign that the line was clear, and the driver accelerated again, and that express chain of goods wagons swept by. I was smothered in smoke, but when it cleared I could see the dispatcher standing gazing after the vanishing trucks as the locomotive whirled up the snow and sucked it along in its wake, a small snow-storm always towed along behind the last wagon, decorated with bits of paper and twigs and leaves ...

And then came the midday interval. I warmed up some soup for myself on the stove in a blue pan, and set the entry signal for the motor-trolley, and Mr Hubička put up his feet on the telegraph table and stared through the window at the blue sky.

'Who's travelling in that trolley, didn't they say?' he asked.

'The track superintendent, they told me,' I answered, stirring my spoon round in the blue pan. Then very quietly the door opened, and somebody came in; I caught a glimpse of grey trousers, polished boots, a winter greatcoat.

'And a very nice life of it you seem to have here,' said the newcomer.

'Not bad,' I said, and went on sipping my soup, and Mr Hubička kept his feet on the telegraph table, and went on gazing at the sky.

'Do you know who I am?' asked the stranger.

'Yes,' I said, 'you've come for the consignation note, you're from the cattle.'

'I could be,' agreed the newcomer. 'And where's your station-master?'

'In the pigeon-loft,' I said.

At that the stranger let out a terrifying bellow.

'Pigeon-loft? More like a bear-garden he keeps here! But do you know who I am?' he demanded again, and answered himself: 'I'm Traffic Chief Slušný!'

Now by this time I'd gathered quite a lot from having listened to station-masters and dispatchers talking, and if they so much as touched on the subject of Traffic Chief Slušný, the very mention of him gave them the shakes. I leaped up, with the pan and spoon still in one hand, and with the other I saluted and presented myself:

'Graduate trainee Miloš Hrma reporting on duty, sir!'

'Put down that pan!' roared the Traffic Chief, and hit out at my blue pan, which fell to the floor, and the Traffic Chief gave it such a kick that it flew clanging under the cupboard. And I stood there at the salute, but Dispatcher Hubička remained all this time seated in his chair with his feet still on the telegraph table, as though terror of the Traffic Chief had paralysed him. And under the window I caught a fleeting glimpse of Mr Lánský hurrying by, and then he came bustling into the office, just as he was; just as he'd scurried down from the pigeon-loft, bareheaded, he saluted and reported for his station.

'At ease!' said the Traffic Chief in a soft, mild voice; and then he carefully examined the stationmaster's old service jacket, covered with pigeondroppings, lingered with delight on the single button left on it, walked all round him and studied his soiled trousers.

'I thought ... ' began the station-master

'He thinks, too?' the Traffic Chief asked me softly.

'Yes, sir,' I said.

'Yes?' marvelled the Traffic Chief. 'And do you know that I had proposed that this chief assistant should be promoted to traffic inspector?'

I shrugged my shoulders.

'Listen, would you like to become a traffic inspector?' he asked the station-master, above whose face a feather was hovering.

'Yes,' sighed Mr Lánský, and the feather fluttered upwards and floated over his forehead.

'And to go on driving the goslings in this fashion?'

'No,' sighed Mr Lánský, and the feather again fluttered like a white question-mark.

'We'll talk about this in Hradec. But a fine station, and that's the truth!' roared the Traffic Chief, and with one swipe swept the dispatcher's boots from the table. 'Do you know who's in the trolley? The commission which has come to consider whether we lodge a criminal charge against this gentleman here, for a felonious infringement of personal liberty ... or deal with him only under the disciplinary regulations!' and he pointed to Dispatcher Hubička.

The station-master opened the door into his own office, hopefully displaying the beautiful Persian carpet with its red and blue flowers, the mahogany table, the palm spreading its leaves like an umbrella, the Turkish smoking table and stools, but the Traffic Chief only shook his head.

'Like master, like man!' he said.

And then in came Councillor Zednicek, who had brought a brief-case with all the documents, and laid out several photographs on the telegraph table, the photographs of all those station stamps decorating the behind of Virginia Svatá, our telegraphist. And the station-master was constantly begging to be allowed to go and change his clothes, insisting that he had a best uniform, but Traffic Chief Slušný wouldn't let him; he had to stay and act as clerk of the court. And then in came Virginia, too; I wouldn't even have recognized her, the way those stamps and the scandal had set her on her feet, somehow she'd grown beautiful, and her eyes had a new depth, so much so that my head swam when she offered me her hand and laughed into my eyes, and told me that she might even be going into films, there was a film company already interested in her.

First of all Councillor Zednicek spread out his

pocket map of Europe, so that he could use it as an introduction, and expound the military situation of the German armies. When he unfolded the map, holes appeared in it. This was because Councillor Zednicek carried this map in his pocket so persistently that he had worn it out at the folded corners. But every one of those holes in the map was as big as Switzerland. Zednicek favoured us with his interpretation of the situation in the Carpathians, where von Mansfeld's Fifth Army was engaged, the army in which Zednicek's son Bretislav was also fighting, but on the map the Fifth Army was still stuck fast in one of the worn-away holes; it was a week now since it had got into it, and it still hadn't managed to climb out of the kettle, so Zednicek's son was fighting away somewhere in that hole. Just like his father, Bretislav Zednicek didn't know the German language properly, and had recommended himself to the Germans by excising the Czech accents from his names. Now Councillor Zednicek went on lecturing, and drawing on his little map of Europe, in pencil, circles which in reality were as big as the Black Sea, and these circles represented the nooses which the German army was going to be drawing tight round the enemy any day now. Councillor Zednicek drew in pencil the line of advance of the German armies across Asia Minor into Africa, where he bottled up the British army groups inside one circle, and then he surged across Spain and took the American forces by the neck, and after that the Councillor moved on to deal with the situation in the protectorate, now heading for total commitment, as was demonstrated by the provisions for simplifying education. Museums and exhibitions would be closed, many trains would be stopped, and sport would be indulged in only on Sundays.

'Is this your posterior?' he asked then, and showed a photograph to Virginia.

'It is,' she said, and smiled.

'Who printed those station stamps on you there?' asked Councillor Zednicek, and the station-master wrote down question and answer.

'Dispatcher Hubička,' said Virginia.

'Well, now, Virginia Svatá, tell us how all this happened,' said Councillor Zednicek.

'We were on night duty together, and by midnight I'd already done my nails, and there weren't any trains running, so we got bored,' began Virginia, gazing at the ceiling.

'Slowly, please,' requested the station-master.

'And then Mr Hubička suggested that we should play forfeits ... you know, Simon says thumbs up, Simon says thumbs down, thumbs up ... and I lost first of all my shoes, and then my panties ... ' explained Virginia, following the motions of the pencil with which Mr Lánský was writing down her evidence.

'And who pulled them off?' probed the Councillor.

'Dispatcher Hubička,' she said, and laughed.

And the dispatcher sat in his chair, one leg thrown over the other, his service cap on his knees, his bald patch shining; and the officials from regional headquarters in Hradec, looking from this bald patch of his to our beautiful telegraphist, sighed and shook their heads, and then with increased bias devoted their attention to the occurrence under discussion, from which they were doing their utmost to dredge up a realistic basis for a criminal charge of infringing personal liberty. And I got on with the duty schedule, switching the signals into the clear position and back again to stop, and I could feel the dispatcher following all the trains that passed through the station under my charge, and I knew he was still supervising everything I did.

Dispatcher Hubička had always been my ideal, even back in Dobrovice where he taught me, when with one hand he could establish a connection with one station, and with the other hand telegraph a lading list to another station. And now he sat here as though before a court, and I felt that the Traffic Chief and Councillor Zednicek, yes, the pair of these officials, would have been only too pleased to do to Virginia exactly the same thing Mr Hubička had done, only they were too cowardly, like all the lot of them, they were too much afraid; the only one who was never afraid of anything was Dispatcher Hubička, sitting here now delighting in his notoriety.

'Now, Miss Virginia Svatá, pay particular attention how you answer,' said Councillor Zednicek, getting up from his seat. 'Before Dispatcher Hubička laid you down on the telegraph table, didn't he place some constraint upon you? Didn't he utter threats? Thrust you down there by force?'

'Good gracious, no, why should he? I did it myself. I lay down myself ... suddenly I felt I wanted to lie down there, without anyone making me ... and wait and see what would happen ... ' said Virginia, laughing.

' ... and wait and see ... what ... would ... happen ... ' whispered the station-master, writing it all down.

I ran out on to the platform. There was another close-surveillance transport running through on the main line. All the fellows sunning themselves there on the tanks were young boys, just like myself, some of them even younger; one lot was tossing a green ball about in the sun, and on another tank they were singing: *Ich hab mein Herz in Heidelberg ver-*

loren ... but when they passed by that strafed train on the fifth line they froze, struck motionless. As each wagon came into the vicinity of those shattered coaches, consigned to the workshops for repair, every person aboard it froze, even the cooks stopped peeling potatoes, though these soldiers must surely have seen worse things at home, shattered towns, houses, heaps of dead. But just here, and now, and this, they hadn't been expecting ...

I went into the station and reported the passage of the transport.

Councillor Zednicek was standing at the window. 'There goes our hope. Our youth. To fight for a Free Europe. And what do you get up to here? You print stamps on a telegraphist's behind!' he said, and turned back to the table, where he cast his eyes once more over the photographs and tossed them away.

'Of course,' he said, 'the criminal charge fails; it was not an infringement of personal liberty ... but it is a debasement of German, the state language!' He drew himself up and thumped his fist on the table. 'Half of those stamps are compounded of German words! And that's a disgrace!'

And I went out on the platform and set the signal for the passage of a medical train coming from the front, a set of express coaches transformed into a hospital. And in this mobile sick-bay at which I was gazing, the strangest thing was the human eyes, the eyes of all those wounded soldiers. As though that agony there at the front, the agony they had inflicted on others and which others now were inflicting on them, had turned them into different people; these Germans were more sympathetic than those who were travelling in the opposite direction. They all peered through the windows into the dull countryside so attentively, with such childlike earnestness, as though they were passing through paradise itself, as though in my little station they saw a jewel-box. They gazed as Dispatcher Hubička gazed at the sky. With exactly the same absorption those yellow invalids stared at me, many of them simply turned their heads, others had to hang on to the horizontal bar suspended from the ceiling of the wagon, another was supported by a nurse; and this hospital train was going home, nothing but white beds, decorated with clenched yellow hands and shrunken yellow faces and childlike eyes. The last wagon of the train was an open box-car, and in it two medical orderlies were stripping a corpse of its hospital gown, and then they dropped it on to a heap of stiffening bodies, soldiers who had died on the journey ... and then this hospital train receded into distance; the red tail-lantern gleamed and clinked and tossed and rattled as it went.

'The noblest blood is staking its life for you,' declaimed Councillor Zednicek, standing at the window. 'Did you see that hospital train? And this is how you behave here! But we've finished. Write down the conclusion, station-master! Disciplinary proceedings with Dispatcher Ladislav Hubička.'

And he waved his hand and went out on to the platform, and signalled for the motor trolley to come alongside. Then Virginia took her seat in the trolley beside the Traffic Chief.

I announced this motor trolley. And gave the signal for departure.

'Czechs! You know what they are?' said Councillor Zednicek. 'Grinning beasts!'

The motor-trolley moved away past the strafed train on the fifth line, and Councillor Zednicek glared at those torn roofs and bullet-holes. The station-master went off up the stairs to the first floor, where he proceeded to yell and bang a chair on the floor until plaster began to fall in the office. He hooted into the ventilator shaft:

'A moral swamp! The ancient city of Sodom! Prostitution under police protection, worming its way into cafés and restaurants and offices. One husband forced his wife to go on the streets! Threatened that if she wouldn't toe the line he'd cut up her little boy with a saw. Wiping their horns! Rubbing the velvet off their antlers! Better that God should sound for the last judgment, and make an end of everything!'

And then he tramped about the kitchen again, and stamped, so that we below should know how he suffered through us. An hour later he came down into his own office. In his parade uniform. Meantime they were just leading the last bull up the ramp at the siding; a lorry had brought him in. This one, too, had been led as far as the lorry by a young girl, on his way to the butcher's. As soon as the lorry drove away the bull began to kick up a shindy. The butcher said to his mate: Bohouš, this bastard's going to smash the sides out for us, here's a knife, prick his eyes out! And his assistant, Bohouš, who told us about it himself afterwards in the office, turned round and stretched his arm through the rear window, and with two stabs put out the bull's eyes.

'And he was quiet enough after that, like a lamb,' said Bohouš to us in the office. 'He-he-he! I reckon he didn't want no part in the world after that.'

When the buyers closed the door with a slam after this bull, the station-master woke up. Along the cornice of the window his pigeons were waddling and cooing and bowing to him, but the station-master only frowned at them and shook his head, ran a finger round his collar, and then fell to thinking again, and grew sadder and sadder. He opened the cupboard and looked at his newest uniform, the one he'd never yet worn; and there was the single gold star already sewn on it, rich with gilt embroidery and gold thread, made from the self-same material from which the spray of lime leaves on a general's uniform used to be made in the old days.

He couldn't restrain himself, he rushed through the traffic office, ran up to the first floor and into the kitchen, and to make certain he shouted several times into the ventilator shaft:

'That's my inspector's field gone up my arse!'

Later on, when the passenger trains had gone through, Mr Hubička was once more standing on the platform and gazing into the blue pre-Spring sky, and surely seeing there again the exploit which had brought him celebrity in the whole region administered by the Hradec Králové headquarters, watching our telegraphist, as in a film, lie down all across that immense blue screen, and seeing himself turn up her skirt, and then take one stamp after another, stamps the size of church towers, and print them into her delicate flesh all over her backside. Suddenly he turned and made up his mind, and in the alcove where the levers and handles of the points were, and the distant signal and the station signals, he whispered to me:

'Miloš, we're on night duty again tomorrow, you and I together ... There'll be a goods train passing through our station, twenty-eight wagons of ammunition, they're carrying it in open trucks, and it'll go through here two hours after midnight. And between our station and the next there are no hills, and not a single house. That whole train could blow up, and no damage to anything but the empty air ... '

'Yes ... yes, it could, Mr Hubička, but what with?'

'We shall get everything, all in good time ... '

'Where is this train?'

'It's coming from Třebič tomorrow.'

'Then once again you and I will be keeping a military transport under close surveillance together ... eh?' I laughed, and there in the alcove the twilight began to close in shortly afterwards. The flock of Polish silver-points flew past the window.

W O R D came from the castle that the station-master was invited to Count Kinský's to dinner, and at seven o'clock a groom would come for him. I drew down the blind and switched on the lights in the traffic office. In the station-master's office, although there was electricity there, I lit the oil lamp with the round wick and the green shade. And I went out with Dispatcher Hubička to the trains, and gave them the green light with my lantern as they passed through our station. Mr Lánský came down into his office and brought his baronial gear with him, the grey trousers and huntsman's jacket, and his Schwarzenberg hat with the capercailzie's feather. He left the door open into the traffic office as he dressed in there, and was pleased to be seen at it.

Along the field track from the castle rode a groom on a white horse, and he had another white horse beside him. The stars were palpitating in the sky, and the night was radiant. The frozen snow began to crackle and crunch underfoot. The green lamp gave forth a gentle hissing sound in the station-master's office, where Mr Lánský was studying himself fixedly in the mirror. He was already in his gala clothes, even the doeskin gloves and the Schwarzenberg hat. And the lamp threw upon the ceiling a small white ring, with larger rings radiating outwards from it like the ribs of a skeleton. When I used to stay with my grandmother on holiday, she had just such a lamp shining on her table, and I liked to lie in bed in the evening and look up at the ceiling, at those shadows round the white ring the oil lamp cast there, and, look at it how I chose, I could always see on the ceiling a kind of skeleton, even when I covered my eyes with the counterpane I could still see that ceiling, and the skeleton on it. Once, when I was staring at the ceiling like this, Granny came in with an apron full of fire-wood, and shot the logs with a rattle into the stove. I shrieked: The skeleton's shin-bones have fallen off!

The groom rode on to the station on his white horse, and beside him stepped the saddled white horse he led. Those horses were so white that they gave off light like a flowering bush of jasmine on a summer night. Mr Lánský came out of the office, and the groom jumped down and helped him into the stirrup. The station-master drew on the reins and trotted over to the pigeon-loft, and called up:

'Go to sleep! I'll come back to you again. Your station-master's coming back! Go to sleep, my children!'

The Polish silver-points cooed, and beat their wings against the lattice of the lowered flight-hatch, and the station-master rode away on his horse, accompanied by the groom. He crossed the tracks, and the two white horses trotted along the hard field path; you could hear the ring of their hooves, but their whiteness merged into the whiteness of the snowy plane, and all that was to be seen was an absurd rear view of the station-master and the groom, those dark clothes and splayed figures sitting, as it were, on empty air.

Dispatcher Hubička drew out the graphs of the time-table, coiled up in a roll like linen or silk. He unrolled it, leaned over it and went through the schedule with a pencil.

I drew aside the little green curtain and sold tick-ets, and out of the dimness of the waiting-room the travellers emerged, bought their tickets and again returned to their dark corners. They didn't want to go out into the frosty air, and they always judged by the dispatcher when their train was coming in. Sometimes I behaved in a rather malicious way to my passengers; the train would be still half an hour distant, but I put on my coat and turned up my collar and went out on to the platform, as though I'd gone to await the imminent arrival of their train; and the passengers would all come flocking out after me, but all I did was to walk up and down a bit, and then I placed my lantern beside the track and went back into the warm office, and the passengers, when they were frozen through, came back to the stove in the waiting-room, from which they turned unfriendly glances on me.

Our station-master, too, sometimes made use of the shadows and the darkness of the night hours, put on his rubber galoshes, and prowled about the station in the night to have a look at what his dis-patchers were doing. Phew! ... once he caught me sleeping after midnight. I was sitting on a chair with my chin on my chest, asleep, while Mr Lánský stood at the rail by the pigeon-hole in the waiting-room, and watched me over the top of the green curtain, and then softly, in his rubber galoshes, he came round by the platform, silently opened the door, silently stood over me and gloated, and then he grabbed me by the shoulder and shook me, and I was so fast asleep that I thought I was at home and it was morning, and I said: What's the time, Dad? and the station-master shouted: This is your station-master, not your dad. And we're on duty! Dad indeed! And then he sent a report to Hradec, and I got a black mark.

The passenger train drew in to the station; I went out on to the platform, and the passengers came flocking out of the waiting-room as the train came steaming slowly in. On the step of the second coach Masha was standing. Her white scarf shone in the night, she had her service lamp on her breast and her conductor's clippers on a strap round her wrist, and just as always, even that time when we were painting the fence all round the workshops, she was as clean and fresh at the end of a shift as if she'd just come on duty.

She jumped down from the step, and when she stretched out her foot she showed little black shoes and white socks, the dimples twinkled in her cheeks, and her face glowed in the blue night as if she had just polished it right to the ears with the corner of a towel. She offered me an apple, and I stood holding my lantern in one hand and the apple in the other, and Masha pressed herself against me and took me in her arms, she was stronger than I, and her cheeks smelled of milk, she pressed herself against me so hard that her little oil lamp warmed my breast, and the flame burned right through into my heart, and she whispered to me :

'Miloš, Miloš, I do love you, I love you so much! All that ... what happened ... that was my fault, I've been asking the girls how to do it, I asked the older ones, everything will surely be all right again, surely, you'll see, I know now how to go about it ... you know?'

And she moved away a step, took her time-table from her pocket, opened it and held out to me a photograph I'd never seen before. I could feel in my fingers how worn it was from much handling ... It was my photograph, the one I gave her that time when we were painting the fence red, the photograph of a boy in a white sailor suit. I turned it over, and there gummed to it was another photograph: I knew at once who it was there gummed to me, it was a childhood photograph of Masha, also in a sailor blouse, and these two pictures stuck together were trimmed into an oval shape.

'Miloš, when will you come over and see us, when?' she asked.

'The day after tomorrow, if you like,' I stammered.

And then it was time for me to whistle number nine in the signal code: Guards, take your places! and the conductresses with raised lamps gave the return signal that they were ready, and I lifted my green lantern, and the train began to move, and Masha pressed herself to me again, clinging to me as closely as those two childhood photographs of ours had had to cling in order to cleave to each other. And Masha kissed me, and then she seized the iron rail and swung herself up on to the footboard, her service lamp gleaming bluish on her breast, and I stood there stricken dumb, because I knew, I was quite sure that I was a real man, I'd been able to convince myself of that, and then, too, I'd felt myself, yes, I was a man, all right, but then how could such a thing happen as had happened to me, that when it came to the point with Masha I wilted like a lily?

The last time I'd seen her was when she came to visit me in the hospital. She bent over my bed, she had on her blue coat with the silver buttons, and when this coat stooped over me the buttons shone like the lights of lamps over a bridge, and she kissed me, but the first thing that happened was that her black service whistle fell out of her breast pocket and hit me in the teeth, and after that she sat down on my bed on my bandaged hand. But soon she had to go away; there was a patient there who had just come round out of narcosis, and he wanted to get up, but he was strapped in, and he shouted: Max, let go the handle-bars, let goooooo, Maaaaxx! And he tore one hand out of the straps and groped under his bed and grabbed a glass urinal there, and with terrible strength he hurled it from him, and it flew clean across the whole room and smashed against the wall by which I was lying, and the urine as it splashed everywhere spattered Masha; she went away with drops shimmering in her hair. She blew me a kiss from the doorway, and all I could do was look at her; and then, when I came out of the hospital, I looked all round, but nobody came to meet me.

I was sad that day, because lying next to me was a fifteen-year-old girl. She'd found in the cupboard a present her parents had bought for her, it was a pair of felt boots, and she couldn't resist putting them on and going off to Prague in them, but there among the rocks by Satalice this train she was in collided with another passenger train, and the seats were rammed together in such a way that the girl's feet were crushed. When she came out of the anaesthetic she was all the time crying: Put my boots in the cupboard, please, my boots ...

So I came out of the hospital alone. When I looked into the shop windows I couldn't recognize myself, I was looking for my own face but it wasn't there, as if I'd become somebody else ... until I stood alone in front of my own image in a show-case; I almost sniffed at myself, and yet still I couldn't help thinking that this must be somebody else, but then I lifted a hand, and that fellow in the reflection lifted his hand, too, then I raised the other hand and he did the same; and I looked, and by the railings there was a bricklayer standing, an enormous chap in white clothes all spattered and encrusted with lime. On the paving lay a Minimax fire-extinguisher, and this bricklayer was looking at me and rolling a cigarette in his fingers, then he put it between his lips, struck a match, and sheltering the match in the little basket made by his palms, he leaned forward and lit up, but all the time looking at me, just as though that door in the little hotel in Bystřice by Benešov was in between us, a door opened just a chink, where I had set my eye to the crack from one side, and this bricklayer from the other ... At the time it had seemed to me as if someone from outside had reached for the same latch at the same instant as I. And now I knew that this old giant of a bricklayer in the lime-whitened clothes was God in disguise ...

Through the station rolled several goods trains, then a passenger train; through the chinks in the guard's van sprouted streaks of light, as sometimes fine hairs do from the crotches of the girls' swim-suits at the bathing-beaches. The firemen fanned away with their shovels under the coal-holder, light splashed into the night, and the moving bodies of the firemen cast moving shadows on the walls of the tender, the entry and departure signals alternately changed from red to green, the luminous signs on the points showed a white symbol, a narrow vertical oblong — the symbol for a through line is a horizontal oblong — meaning that the line was switched away into the curve, and then there, where the siding ended at Liverpool, a blue lamp burned clearly all through the night. The arms of the distant signals clanged as the light changed, the office was full of the ticking of instruments, and now and then the buzz of a telephone, connected up by mistake; the block-system echoed to the rattle of wheels released as the tracks were opened, and in the middle of all this humming activity Dispatcher Hubička paced to and fro, full of anxiety about that close-surveillance train of his which was to bring twenty-eight wagons of ammunition after midnight.

He followed that train on the graph, and then listened, looked out on the platform from darkness into darkness, and peered into the waiting-room, while I thought about Masha, and grew sick with dread, for how would it turn out when it came to the point for us again?

And now I, too, was standing on the platform, and I, too, looked up into the night sky, and there I saw a film of my own; across the whole of the sky I laid Masha down, just as Hubička had laid Virginia on the telegraph table, and piece by piece I drew the clothes off her, but when Masha lay there naked across the sky, I didn't know what to do with her next. I knew, but I still had no practical experience of it, that is, because I'd never yet been in any woman, except the time when I was in my mother's womb, but I couldn't remember anything about that ...

And then I heard the station-master's wife coming down the stairs, a candle in one hand, and in the other a pot full of poultry-rusks, going down into the cellar, where the gander was gaggling in alarm. I stood on the platform, and through the square of the window I looked into the cellar, where Mrs Lánská and her shadow stooped together as she took a rusk from the pot, and then opened the gander's bill and pushed in the rusk, and then held his beak fast, like shutting a clasp-knife, and with her fingers stroked the bread down his throat into his crop. And again she moistened a rusk in water and went on feeding the gander, in spite of his resistance.

'I'll be right back, take over for me,' I said to Mr Hubička. 'I've got to go for a minute.'

And then I groped my way with one hand round the curve of the wall, and planted my boots step by step down the winding stairs, and quietly opened the door into the cellar.

'Mrs Lánská, don't be afraid,' I said. 'It's me, Miloš.'

'What is it?' she asked, startled, and remained standing with a rusk in her fingers, and the light of the candle, burning behind her, shone through her grey curls, and I could see her careworn face; a kind of Cinderella she was, while the station-master was off playing Baron Lánský of the Rose.

'It's me, Miloš,' I said. 'Mrs Lánská, I've come to you for advice. You see, it's like this, the day after tomorrow I'm going to see my young lady, Masha, that conductress, you know? And she's sure to ... to want me to ... to ... you know?'

'I don't know,' she stammered, and leaned down to moisten a rusk, and opened the gander's beak.

'You do know,' I said. 'Please don't pretend you don't. I've come to ask you for your advice ... The thing is, I *am* a man, all right, but then when I've got to show that I am, then again, all at once, I'm not a man ... According to the books I've got *ejaculatio praecox*, you know?'

'I don't know,' she repeated, and again dabbled a rusk in the water.

'But you do know,' I said. 'Right now, this minute, I believe ... yes, there, ... please, I'm a man now ... feel!'

'Holy Virgin!' whispered Mrs Lánská. 'But Miloš, I'm already in the change ... '

'In what?'

'In the change ... But this is awful!' and she shook so much that she overturned the pot with the poultry-rusks.

I kneeled down and began to gather them up, and Mrs Lánská began picking them up, too, and while we were at it I told her why I'd slashed my wrists that time, because I wilted in Uncle Noneman's studio, the studio with the notice saying: FINISHED IN FIVE MINUTES, because I was finished even before I began. And the station-master's wife was silent now, holding the gander by the beak.

'Please feel, Mrs Lánská,' I said.

'All right, Miloš, I will,' she said, and she stooped, with her shadow stooping behind her on the wall, and blew out the candle.

'Well, am I a man?' I asked.

'Yes, Miloš, you are,' she said.

'Yes ... but then, Mrs Lánská, what next? Wouldn't you be kind enough to teach me? Please, if only you would ... At the psychiatric clinic Doctor Brabec told me that I ought to rub the velvet off my antlers with some older lady ... '

'But Miloš, I'm in the change already, I don't want to have anything to do with all that any more, really, I do understand, and if I were younger ... Holy Virgin, what's got into you all on this station? First it's Dispatcher Hubička with those stamps, and now you rubbing the velvet off your antlers ... But everything will be all right the day after tomorrow, you'll see, you're a man, all right, very much so ... '

Through the window of the cellar I saw Mr Hubička come out on to the platform, spread out his legs and look up at the sky, and I knew quite well that it wasn't Virginia who was spread out there now, jutting her bottom across the whole heaven; no, what was silently approaching there was a goods train with twenty-eight wagons, which would suddenly vanish to give place to a gigantic cloud spouting into the air, growing and growing, tall as the cloud-castles in the sky before a summer storm, and even taller ...

'Are you angry with me, Mrs Lánská?' I asked.

'No, Miloš, I'm not angry, all this is just human ... ' she said.

And she felt her way along the wall and climbed heavily from step to step, up to the first floor, and then she walked to and fro through the kitchen and the living-room, just as the station-master walked when he couldn't control himself, and dared not tell us to our faces what he had against us, and therefore went and poured it all into the ventilator shaft, and then came down again purged and calm, because if he hadn't yelled into the ventilator-shaft he would have had to roar at his wife. Terrible things he said to her, everything that was unclean in him he poured out on her, and in a little while he'd forgotten all about it; so that he never had to slash his veins, like me, nor turn up his telegraphist's skirt and print stamps on her bottom, and I saw in advance that our station-master couldn't go mad, either. He had a completely effective system of mental hygiene in this act of yelling everything into the ventilator shaft, and the odd bit now and then into his wife, who knew when to give him one over the chops with a wet rag, or rip back at him with some terribly rude retort, which would collapse him just as effectively as that quarterly clout, after which he was like a man just waking up.

As for Dispatcher Hubička, the more the evening drew on towards midnight, the more uneasy he became; he was for ever jumping up, stopping abruptly, and listening. I saw that every moment he was expecting the door to open and reveal a hand, holding out to him a message or a package.

When the station-master's clock struck twelve, I said:

'What a beautiful chime that clock has!'

And the door opened as though caught in a draught, and in came a young woman in an unbuttoned *loden* hunting coat, beneath which we could see a Tyrolean blouse embroidered with green oak-shoots and acorns. She wore a grey skirt and white wool stockings, and bootees with protruding tongues. Dressed like our station-master, only the feminine version. And she was carrying a small, wrapped parcel.

'*Bitte,*' she said, '*ich muss nach Kersko.*'

'To Kersko!' I said. 'Then you'll have to wait until morning, that's across the river.'

'But I must get to Kersko,' she insisted.

'It's a long way. Who're you going to there?' I asked.

'I have a friend,' she said, and laughed, pointing a finger at me. 'You are the duty dispatcher?'

'Oh, no, this is the duty dispatcher ... ' I said.

'You are Dispatcher Hubička?' she asked him.

'*Ja,*' he said.

'And him?' she pointed at me.

'*Mein Freund,*' said the dispatcher.

'Miloš Hrma,' I introduced myself.

'Viktoria Freie.' She bowed, and held out her hand.

'Viktoria Freie?' repeated Hubička in wonder.

And I knew that this was the word we were waiting for, I knew it, and I knew that Viktoria Freie was the hand that brought the message and the charge; but at this moment that charge brought no comfort to Dispatcher Hubička, in fact rather the opposite, he grew even paler; this apparition had knocked him quite off-balance. I could see that he hadn't the least stirring of desire, that he wasn't even looking at this handsome woman's behind or breasts,

in the way he usually had of undressing a woman
with his eyes. And this Tyrolean girl, now that I came
to look at her, was simultaneously both a bummie
and a buster.

I went out on to the platform and gave a goods
train the signal to pass through, sprinkling it with
green light. And when I came back and notified the
next station of the time when this train had passed
through my station, the little parcel had vanished.

And Viktoria yawned and stretched, and made
eyes at me, and all at once I felt such trust in her
that when she said she would like to get an hour's
sleep, I opened the door into the station-master's
office, just as Mr Hubička had done in Dobrovice the
night he tore that oilcloth couch, and she went in,
and I brought her coat, and laid it on the couch.
The green lamp-shade shone tenderly, and I could hear
how uneasy the pigeons still were in their loft, even
more so than when the station-master rode away; it
sounded as though a marten or a weasel had got in
there with them, they cooed and beat their wings
in such alarm.

'My name is Miloš Hrma,' I stammered. 'You know,
I slashed my veins because I'm supposed to be suffer-
ing from *ejaculatio praecox*. But it isn't true. Oh,
it's true that I wilted like a lily with my girl, but
between you and me, I really am a man ... '

'You mean you've never had a woman yet?' asked
Viktoria, marvelling.

'No, I haven't, I only tried, and that's why I
wanted to ask you if you could advise me ... '

'Really, you've never had anyone yet?' she repeated, growing every moment more astonished.

'No, nobody, because Masha ... well, she did come
in to me at Uncle Noneman's studio in Karlín, so I
suppose I did have Masha with me, but I didn't

have anything with her, because, as I say, I wilted like a lily.'

'Then you really haven't ever had a woman yet,' she said, and she smiled at me, and she had dimples, just like Masha, and her eyes grew soft, as though she was lost in wonder at some unexpected happiness, or had found some precious thing, and with her fingers she began to play in my hair as if I'd been a piano. Then she looked at the closed door into the traffic office, and leaned over the table, turned down the wick, and with an audible breath blew out the lamp.

And then she touched me, and drew me with her to the station-master's couch, and dropped on to it and drew me down upon her, and then she was kind to me, like when I was a little boy and my mother used to dress and undress me, she even allowed me to help her pull up her skirt, and then I felt her raise and part her legs, planting those Tyrolean shoes of hers on the fabric of the station-master's couch, and then all in an instant I was glued to Viktoria, just as I was glued to Masha in the photographs in the sailor suits, and I was overwhelmed by a flood of light growing ever more brilliant, I was marching, marching uphill, the whole earth shook, and there was the rolling of thunder and storm, and I had the impression that it didn't come from me or from Viktoria's body, but from somewhere outside, that the whole building was shaking to its foundations, and the windows rattling. I could hear even the telephones ringing in honour of this my glorious and successful entry into life, and the telegraphs began to play Morse signals of their own accord, as sometimes happened in the traffic office during storms; even the station-master's pigeons seemed to me to be cooing in unison, and at last the very horizon soared and blazed with the colours of fire, and the station building shook again, and shifted a little on its foundations ...

And then I felt Viktoria's body rear up in an arch, I heard her metal-tipped shoes slice into the oilcloth couch, I heard the cloth tear and tear endlessly, and out of somewhere unknown there surged through me from the very nails of all my fingers and toes, and converged upon my brain, an exultant convulsion, everything was suddenly white, then grey, then brown, as though hot water had showered over me and changed into cold, and in my back I felt a pleasant pain, as though someone had jabbed me there with a bricklayer's trowel.

I opened my eyes. Viktoria was still playing in my hair with a finger, and sighing. And I saw, through a chink in the blind, the red and amber colours of far-away fires soaring high on the horizon, as though kindled by intermittent lightning. And the station-master's pigeons were cooing in terror and flying about the pigeon-loft, striking against walls and roof and falling to the floor, beating frightened wings.

Viktoria Freie sat up and listened. She smoothed her hair, and said:

'There's a terrible air-raid somewhere.'

I opened the window and tugged at the blind, which rushed upwards with a sucking sound. Far away beyond the hill burst out more and more fires, the entire horizon was red and frayed over there beyond the hill, towards the centre of some distant disaster.

'That could well be Dresden,' she said, and rose and combed out her hair, and the comb running through her hair gave out a strange sound. I thought of her lissom body, which I could suddenly imagine flying on a trapeze.

'What are you?' I asked.

'An artiste,' she said, inclining her head as she drew the comb through her thick hair. 'Before the war we used to have a show called: The Rainbow Palette of Aerial Attractions.'

I sat down on the couch and quietly felt across the oilcloth. The couch was almost torn in half. The seaweed stuffing was bulging out. Through the station went a goods train, spitting sparks from its chimney. Viktoria stood at the window and combed those sparks out of her hair. Then along the field track we could see two riders silhouetted against the ruddy horizon.

I stood up, and for the first time in my life I felt myself at peace.

'Thank you,' I said.

'Thank *you*!' she said, and she picked up her coat and went into the traffic office and looked at the clock. She sighed, and put up a hand under her blouse to adjust her breast in her brassière. And out she went on to the platform, where Dispatcher Hubička stood with his legs spread wide, gazing at the sky. For a while they talked together. Then she came back, and said:

'And now I really must get on to Kersko,' and she laughed, and walked away past the station-master's little garden, and striding along the alley of limes, she vanished between the houses.

When Mr Lánský rode up on his white horse, he jumped down lightly and tossed the reins to the groom, who chirruped at his own horse and trotted away home again.

The station-master went straight to the pigeon-loft and called up: 'My little May kittens, what's the matter, what's frightened you so? What have they done to you, then? My winged children! Your station-master's come back to you! There, there!'

And then he tramped gaily into the traffic office, reversed a chair and plumped himself down astride it, and said:

'The Prince sends you his regards, Hubička. Baron Betmann Holweg brought those photographs of Virginia. All the gentry are enthusiastic, and want to see you. The Count himself asked me to tell you, Hubička, that he envies you, he says he'd never have thought of that. He invites you to visit the castle, Hubička, next week. I had to give the company at table a full account of how it all happened ... '

He got up, the telegraph was calling our station. *'Bahnhofsperre Dresden, Pirna, Bautzen ... '*

The station-master went out on to the platform, and shouted in the direction where the thunderous reverberations still continued, where the sky was coloured red:

'You shouldn't have set out to make war on the whole world!'

DISPATCHER Hubička switched on the shaded lamp on the telegraph table, opened the telegraph diary close to the corner of the table, and made a sign to me that he wanted to show me something in the reports, but I knew at once that this would really be something quite different. The dispatcher was anxious and haggard, and when he pointed with his pencil at an item in the reports, the point of the pencil trembled and scribbled on the paper like a cardiograph. Carefully he opened the drawer, and I was supposed to be looking at the last entry, but instead I squinted into the drawer. Only the cone of light from the table lamp shone in the traffic office, and at the bottom of the drawer gleamed a revolver, and beside it was some object resembling a battery torch, only instead of glass it had something like a watch, which was ticking quietly.

'Miloš,' said the dispatcher in a whisper, and went on indicating and underlining an entry in the diary, 'Miloš, the best thing will be to stand on the platform and throw it into the central wagon. We'll set the signal at stop for this train, and then at the last moment give him the green — that'll slow him down for us.'

'That's true,' I said. I felt that at all the windows of the waiting-room, and all the chinks in the blind, everywhere there might be eyes watching us; for that reason I took the pencil and also underlined an entry in the telegraph diary as I whispered:

'But you remember how the arm of the signal dropped? Just as that express mail was coming through? You know what? I'll do the same again. I'll climb out on the signal and drop this explosive from above, like this, lean over and let it fall into the middle wagon, and then slip down again, and we shall see what that'll do ... Where is this close-surveillance transport of ours?'

'It's passed through Poděbrady, half an hour and it'll be here,' the dispatcher spat out huskily, and with his belly he closed the drawer, and nonsensically signed himself in on a page of the diary. 'Aren't you afraid?'

'No, I've never been so calm ... Aaaahhh!' I said 'I'm a man, I'm a man just like you, Mr Hubička, a man, and that's wonderful, everything's fallen off my shoulders.' I picked up the long scissors from the table and clashed them shut. 'That's how I've cut myself off from the past,' I laughed, and picked up the telephone.

'It's the express mail,' I said, and reported it to the signal-box. 'Set the points for the mail, number fifty-three, sixty-one.'

And I withdrew the key from the block-system and went out into the night, where the horizon was still smeared with that great stain, as though the sun had set there only a few minutes ago. Lightly I tossed over the levers of the station signals and the distant. Never had my head been so clear, it was as though my mother constantly soothed and caressed me, like when I was a child and she'd chased away a bad dream from me. Dispatcher Hubička paced the office, staring at the floor; he didn't even come out to look at the sky any more. Had I seen it for myself in advance, just as he had, this heavy responsibility for how the affair would turn out? And even if well, what then? But it wasn't of that I was thinking — not that it wasn't incumbent on me to consider it, and I had considered it, right through to the end — but now that had ceased to interest me, I was concentrated all on this one consideration, that I should drop that thing from the signal precisely into the one wagon which would ensure that the whole train should be blown into the air; there was nothing else I wished for, nor could I see anything else in the sky, except that ever-mounting cloud which would suck into itself the shattered fragments of trucks and tracks and sleepers.

And I thought of this, too, that I ought to have been thinking on these lines long ago, hadn't I good reason? ... ever since they had run over my grandfather, who went marching out alone to meet them, alone against an army corps, with outstretched hands and a hypnotist's power of the mind, to force the Germans to turn and go back where they came from. And just the same, even if Grandfather's head was mashed into the tracks of the tank, it surely was nothing else but Grandfather's spirit that was constantly forcing army corps after army corps, tank after tank, soldier after soldier, back into the heart of Germany, back to the place from which they had come pouring in the attack, and to which the Russian armies were sweeping them home ... But I had forgotten about Grandfather, because if I had thought of him earlier I might have attempted other things. As it was, in twenty minutes my train would be here, my train loaded with ammunition, and I should have the opportunity of achieving something great, for I was no wilted lily now. I should never have dreamed that there could be such reserves of strength in me, just as I should never have guessed that Dispatcher Hubička would be growing every moment more anxious and tense; he couldn't even pace any longer, he was standing all the time over the block-system, and listening to the telephones which were reporting the progress of our close-surveillance train.

I went into the office, opened the drawer, and slipped the bomb into the pocket of my coat, while Dispatcher Hubička covered my movements with his body. The revolver I put into my other pocket, and then I ran a finger through the items in the telegraph diary and signed my name, and put away the pencil in the drawer.

Mr Hubička went to the blackboard on which were inscribed from yesterday, in chalk, all the close-surveillance trains, the series of twenty military transports which were to attempt to sustain the broken front-line. He pointed a finger at it, and whispered:

'Miloš, I'll set the time mechanism for you at the last moment ... '

'Yes ... but there's the mail coming in now.'

And I went out on to the platform as the fast mail steamed into the station and stopped, and the train chief jumped down.

'Ghastly, the whole of Dresden's *kaput*,' he said.

And after him came clambering down out of the cars a crowd of people who looked as though they'd escaped from a concentration camp, for they all had on striped trousers, but when they came into the office we could see that these were people in striped pyjamas, with only coats thrown over them, just as they had got away with their bare lives, and they all had fixed eyes that never blinked. The train chief collapsed into a chair and mopped his forehead.

'The whole of Dresden's one torch. This lot climbed into my vans,' he said, and got up heavily, as a weary horse gets to its feet. For a moment he leaned both fists on the telegraph table, then he folded his arms and remained standing, his head drooping. It looked as if he'd dropped off to sleep. And those Germans stood in just the same way, staring at the ground; maybe they were seeing those last moments when they had leaped out of their windows into gardens and streets, everything cut off from them by falling trees and walls and beams. All those Germans had long arms, hanging now almost to their knees, and all this time not one of them blinked, as though horror had cut off their eyelids. And I had no pity for them, I who had wept over every kid that ever was slaughtered, and everything that suffered distress, I could find no pity now for those Germans.

When I was still in the hospital with those wrists of mine I used to go and visit my distant aunt, and this Aunt Beatrice had been a nurse in the hospital for fifty years, and was in charge of the ward where burned people were brought together to die; they were mostly soldiers now, brought from the front line in oil, so that they were almost amphibians when they came; and my Great-aunt Beatrice made vegetable soup for them, and when any of them had too much pain she gave them morphia injections, and I used to go there to see her, because Great-aunt Beatrice had a tranquillizing effect on everybody. She was so huge and strong that everyone, as soon as she looked at him, was steeped in calm, perhaps because she'd been in that department for so many years ... and yet, when I was in tears over those German soldiers, when I saw their sweethearts and wives come to visit them, and watched the soldiers from their oil-baths making their last dispositions and recommending their wives whom to marry next when they were gone, and how to manage everything with the children and the property, I wanted to get up and go, but Great-aunt Beatrice pressed me back in my chair and went on slicing carrots and celery and chopping parsley. She sliced away and sang softly to herself, for every change of name a change of melody ... That *Gefreiter* Schulte's going to die tomorrow ... to the tune of: 'On the Prague bridge growing, rosemary is blowing' ... and her knife sliced away at the carrots and parsley and celery ... and she knew that tomorrow she would give a slightly larger dose of morphia to Lance-Corporal Schulte and shorten his agony by a few days, for already he was taking his leave ... and the next day again she would be singing softly: *Ober-leutnant* Ditie, tomorrow he'll be dead ... to the tune of: 'My girl gave to me a little gilded ring' ...

And she sliced vegetables, and I looked at the young men in the oil-baths; they all looked as if they were simply bathing, and I had no wish at all for them to be dead tomorrow, I wished that they could come back to those wives and sweethearts of theirs with whom they were talking for the last time, for when anyone was sent down here to Aunt Beatrice, you could say it was already all up with him. But now, as these Dresdeners came flocking here out of their city, I could no longer pity them, nobody could pity them, except they themselves. And those Germans knew it. The train chief got up and said to the Germans:

'*Sollten Sie am Arsch zu Hause sitzen.*'

And he went out on to the platform, and raised his hand, and the engine began to move, and the train chief jumped into the service wagon.

'God must have sent these Germans here to us,' whispered the dispatcher hoarsely. 'They'll be our witnesses, if anything ... ' he spluttered, and from the track I heard the acoustic signal echoing from one linesman's hut to the next, a little hammer beating on a cracked bell, and I knew at once that this was my train. I went into the office and the dispatcher was holding the telephone, and by his extreme pallor I saw that this was indeed the train we had under close surveillance.

I drew out the key. The Germans were standing round the stove, motionless still, like statues on the plague column in our square. Now one of them burst out weeping, in such a strange way, almost cooing, like the station-master's pigeons when the raid disturbed them, and then his weeping became human, and only then did his body relax. And the other Germans began to blow their noses, and then they all burst into tears, every one in a different way, but fundamentally this was human crying, lamentation over what had happened. And one of them was cooling his forehead against the wall, and now suddenly blood began to flow from his nose, and all at once he slid down to the floor, and left a red streak all down the wall.

Dispatcher Hubička looked at me, he had his cap pulled so low over his forehead that he had to raise his chin.

I ran out to the alcove, and set the distant signal and the arrival signal at all clear, but the departure signal I left at stop. The dispatcher came to me there, and I drew from my pocket that little instrument, and he shone his torch on it and adjusted the rings, as though he were sharpening the focus of a camera.

And all the while the pigeons were cooing distressfully, unable to sleep; we could hear their wings beating against the wall.

Then Dispatcher Hubička held his hand out to me,

cold and moist; it might have been a fish he was offering me. And I walked along the line.

A long cloud coursed across the moon, and began to shed a spatter of frozen snow, and I turned round, and saw in the distance the shaded light of a locomotive. The moon sailed out of the snow-cloud, and in the frosty night the planes of the fields glittered, and again I heard all those frozen crystals ticking, as though in every one of them swung a prismatic second hand. Then I climbed up the standard of the signal as on a ladder. And again a cloud passed across the moon, and again began to sprinkle snow, fine as midges. I straddled the lamp. The locomotive drew into the station and whistled grievously because it had no signal for a clear line. Then I felt the wing of the signal rising, it lifted my hand with it, and the lamp changed its red light into green. And in this all-clear position the arm formed a sufficient cover for me, because it was bigger than I.

The locomotive whistled, I saw the dispatcher give them the signal to proceed with his green lantern, and I sat there on the signal lamp in the falling snow; I could feel the frozen flakes pecking at me, and see how thickly the snow was coming down now. I never moved, I was already holding that thing in my hand, and I could hear the ticking of the mechanism vibrating through me. And then the locomotive passed by, it was covered from above by a cloth, so that the dive-bombers shouldn't locate it from a distance when the firemen were at work. Then came one wagon after another, low, open wagons, and on them the gunpowder in cases, bedded down in layers of straw, three, four, five wagons, I counted them. The moon was veiled behind those flying clouds from which the snow was falling now so thickly, and yet this moon was always visible, like a drowned hoop at the bottom of a brook rushing through a shallow trough. Seven, eight, nine, and the snow was falling so heavily that for a while I could see neither the locomotive nor the last wagon of this train; eleven, twelve, thirteen, and then lightly I tossed the instrument I held, like somebody tossing a flower into a stream. I'd counted accurately, and thrown it just as the front of the wagon passed beneath me, and it dropped exactly into the middle of the wagon predestined to receive this tiny thing, which now lay there silently, carrying away this close-surveillance train to its end.

I was watching this fourteenth wagon steadily to the last moment, the wagon and the stain it carried in its heart, until the snow streaked and shrouded it from me, and I intended to sit out those four minutes here aloft, to the end of that measured time I meant to watch from this vantage-point, like a huntsman awaiting here the moment of the kill.

And then I saw the last wagon approaching, with a little hut on the end of it, and out of the hut a long cone of light slashed abruptly and settled upon me, and I drew my revolver, and saw a rifle-barrel glint immediately below me. I fired, and at the same moment somebody fired from the hut, and the torch fell to the ground and gleamed in the gravel-bed, and out of the hut on the train somebody pitched after it, and rolled into the ditch. And I felt a pain in my shoulder, and the revolver dropped from my hand, and I fell head-first, but my coat caught on a hook, and the signal rattled and the green changed to red, and the arm fell into the horizontal position, and I hung head-down and heard my coat gradually tearing. My keys and small change fell out of my pockets and rained past my singing ears, and I saw the train receding into the distance, saw the whole length of it sweep round the curve, showing itself to me wheels upwards, as if it ran across the ceiling of the night, until the red tail lights at its end dwindled into the distance. And in the ditch beside the signal I saw a soldier coiled into a ball, snow was falling on him, he had lost his cap, and he had a bald head ... and my coat slowly tore, and I could feel blood flowing from beneath my shirt down my neck to my head. And then my coat tore clear, and I fell head-first into the black gravel bed saturated with oil and steam.

I fell on my hands, and the corners of a sharp stone tore my palms. Then I rolled into the ditch, right beside that German soldier, who was lying on his back and beginning to march on the spot, all the time he marched steadily, gouging through the snow with his heavy boots right to the frozen soil and turf, and he held himself by the belly and cried.

I put my hand in front of my mouth, and when I coughed I spat out blood. This German soldier had shot me through the lungs, and I him, it seemed, through the belly. Now I realized why Dispatcher Hubička had been hawking and spitting the whole evening. It was as though he had foreseen this my end, because Mr Hubička had never been afraid of anything. This thing had perhaps been stronger than he, everything had, as it were, happened already before it happened ... I looked at the sky, from which the snow came drifting, then I turned over and clawed my way to the soldier, who had begun to cry out, repeating over and over only one word.

'*Mutti, Mutti, Mutti!*' he called, and I watched him and brought up blood, and I knew that this man wasn't calling for his own mother, but for the mother of his children, for he was already bald. When I leaned over him I saw that he was so like Dispatcher Hubička that I was startled. And then he kept clutch-

ing his hands to his belly, and it was as though he was wanting all the time to go away from this shot body of his; steadily he marched on the spot, and with the soles of his heavy military boots he scored through the snow to the frozen clay. I spread out my arms and lay down on my back, blood trickled from the corner of my mouth, and my breast was full of fire. And suddenly I saw what perhaps Dispatcher Hubička had always seen, that I was lost, that all I could do was wait for that train to fly into the air, and if there was nothing else, then in this situation that would have to be enough for me, because there could be nothing in store for me but death, whether I died of this rifle-shot, or whether they found me and the Germans hanged or shot me, according to their custom. And so it dawned on me at last that I had been predestined for another death than the one I had attempted there in Bystřice by Benešov. When it came to the point I was sorry that I had shot this German in the belly, this soldier who still clutched his bowels, and still marched endlessly with those boots of his, and I knew that now nobody could ever help him again, either, for a shot through the belly is mortal, only the death towards which this German marched was a long way off, and it seemed as if he could never hope to reach it this way, for all he was doing was marching on the spot, and in rhythm with his marching he went on repeating:
'Mutti, Mutti, Mutti ... '
Those military boots were gouging into my brain. I rolled over and dragged myself on my elbows right up to those army boots, and with both arms I tried to hold them still, but his feet were so strongly on the move that they shook and jerked me like the levers of some machine. Out of the pocket of my coat I pulled the string I used for tying numbered labels

on to bicycles or prams, when travellers took them with them by train in the luggage van. I wiped away blood, and bound one end of the string round one boot, and when the feet changed step I tied the other boot, too, and for a moment those feet stopped marching and jerked helplessly together, but then by the strength of the machine they broke the string, and scored the earth once more, and even hastened their step, while the soldier cried in a louder voice:

'*Mutti, Mutti, Mutti!*'

And so he reminded me all the more of something I didn't want to think about, of how Mum would be standing behind the curtain in the morning, waiting for me, but I should never again emerge from the lane and turn into the square, and she would never wave the curtain as a sign that she was expecting me, and that she saw me, and that she was happy ... because my Mum can never sleep in peace when I'm on night duty, just as maybe this soldier's wife hasn't been able to sleep since he's been away at the front. Maybe she, too, stands somewhere behind a curtain, and waits for somebody to turn into the street and beckon to her, and it will be this man, who lies here marching on the spot and calling for her, marching and marching, but his march can only end in death.

I clawed my way to him, and called into his ear: '*Ruhe! Ruhe!*'

But this soldier already knew his end; and I, as I laid my hand in the snow to prop myself, felt the cold barrel of the rifle, and I seized it and rolled over on to my side. So the soldier lay there, and I opposite him. I placed the muzzle of the rifle where the heart lies, I get mixed up between right and left, but I worked it out by testing first with one hand and then with the other whether it was possible to write. Yes, now I settled the rifle against the soldier's heart, so that he wouldn't call out any more, so that he would stop tramping through my head. I squeezed the trigger. A shot rang out, and the damped-down fire singed his uniform, I could smell burned cotton and wool, but the soldier only called out even more urgently for his wife, the mother of his children, and marched on the spot with an accelerated pace, as though these were the last few steps, and then only the garden and the house beyond it, the house in which his dearest lived ...

The snow had stopped falling, a lovely moon came out, over the wide countryside the coloured second hands ticked in every flake, and round the neck of this soldier a silver chain gleamed white, and on the chain hung something which he seized in both hands, calling ever more loudly:

'*Mutti! Mutti!*'

And I held the barrel of the rifle to his eye and pressed the trigger; I was lying awkwardly as I did it. And then I heard him fall silent, and I saw his marching feet slowly and quietly arrive, and stop; I was lying on him, and I heard peace and silence enter into him, I heard and felt everything stop, like a machine which has broken down.

Blood was purling out of me, and I'd soiled the soldier's clothes, I pulled out my handkerchief and tried to clean the bloody stain from him, and I was panting and beginning to suffocate, but with all my strength I rolled over and stretched out my hand to grasp the chain the soldier was holding. His face had grown peaceful now, only instead of a right eye he had a burned hole like a blue monocle ... And I tore loose this chain to which the dead man was clinging, and in the light of the moon I saw that it was a little medallion; on one side of it was a green four-leaved clover, and on the other side the inscription: *Bringe*

Glück. But that four-leaved clover hadn't brought any luck either to this soldier or to me. He was a man, too, like me, or like Mr Hubička, like us he hadn't any distinction or rank, and yet we had shot each other and brought each other to death, although surely if we could have met somewhere in civil life we might well have liked each other, and found a lot to talk about.

And then the explosion rang out. And I, who only a little while before had been looking forward to this sight, lay there beside the German soldier, stretched out my hand and opened his stiffening fingers, and put into them the green four-leaved clover that brings luck, while from somewhere away there in the countryside a mushroom cloud soared into the sky, endlessly expanding into greater heights and vaster smoky masses. I heard the pressure of the air rush across the countryside and hiss and whistle through the bare branches of the trees and bushes, I heard it rattle the transfer chains on the signal, and lean on the arm and shake it; but I lay coughing, and felt my blood draining out of me.

To the last moment, before I began to lose the awareness of myself, I held this dead man by the hand, and for his unhearing ears I repeated the words of the chief of that mail train which had brought those wretched Germans from Dresden:

'You should have sat at home on your arse ... '